David Weaver Presents

A Boss's Love

By Jameelah Kareem

Prologue

"Let me get twenty-five dollars on pump four," Rev said as he handed the cashier the cash and pushed over the red Gatorade on the counter.

After the cashier rang him up, Rev headed out to the parking lot. He got to his car and pulled open the gas tank lid. As soon as he picked up the gas pump, he felt a metal object on his left temple. He froze, knowing exactly what it was.

"You fucked up, nigga," a voice said in a low, angry tone.

"You don't gotta do this," Rev pleaded.

"I don't have to, but I want to. Rev, you know the code: snitches get stitches."

Rev didn't know how to react, so he didn't. His mind raced with thoughts of this being the end. He thought about his girlfriend and son and if he would ever see them again. He thought about who this was with a gun to his head. What did he do? Why was someone trying to kill him?

In the few moments that he had these thoughts, he quickly snapped out of it and into survival mode. He tried to turn slowly to get a look at the person, but didn't want to cause them to shoot him. He realized they didn't shoot yet so there was still room for surviving this situation. His gun was under his driver side seat, which would take a little bit of maneuvering to get to, so he thought of an alternative.

His eyes darted to the side to try to get a look at the person and all he could see was all black. A hoodie over their head tied tightly. He realized there were feminine features inside the hoodie and he thought about the voice. A female! He quickly got excited because he knew he could overpower a female, he just wasn't sure if he would be quick enough.

He decided to take the chance. He reached out and quickly tried to grab her arm and get the gun. She grabbed at the gun with her other hand, trying to keep control of its grip. He reached back to punch her and just barely hit her on the side of the face. In that instant, she knew it was time to shoot. Three shots rang out and Rev's body hit the ground. He didn't move. She stared down at his motionless body, hovering above it. She came to her senses and ran off to her car that was still running and sped off. Mission accomplished.

Chapter 1

Questions with no Answers

I couldn't help but stare at her. The blue jeans she wore hugged her wide hips and thick thighs. The white tank top she wore showed her large brown nipples that poked through the front. I caught a glimpse every time she moved and her little black leather jacket slid to the side, exposing them. Around her neck, she wore a small gold cross that dangled and landed on her creamy almond skin. She was perfect and I wanted her. I wanted every inch of her.

I watched her walk over to her girlfriends and excitedly hug each one and kiss them on the cheek. They looked happy to see her, as if they didn't see each other daily. They walked over to the bar and tried to get the bartender's attention and began to order their drinks. My eyes never left her. I had to have this girl.

Her name was Jasmine. I knew her from seeing her around at different clubs and events around the city, but we never really spoke. We knew each other's face and she might even follow me on Instagram, but she never paid me enough attention for me to approach her. I never felt like I was her type. I was confident in myself, but she seemed like the type to only fuck with these 9-5 niggas—the guys who went to college with her and could give her a white picket fence, a baby and a dog. I could offer her all of that, but there was no telling how long it would be before the Feds were banging on the door, taking it all away. I was a street nigga. The kind that didn't give a fuck about anything except the money. Family meant nothing to me. Friends meant nothing to me. Love meant nothing to me. A real street soldier only cared about four things: me, myself and I, and of course the money. I knew she probably wanted some soft nigga to cater to her and treat her good; it wasn't me, but I damn sure wanted to fuck her.

I got up and walked towards her and the group of girls she was with. I threw my plastic cup in the trash can that sat next to the bathroom on the way to the bar. I squeezed through the hot bodies that crowded around the bar and stood next to her. My body pressed up against hers and I tried not to get too excited. The side of her ass rubbed my thigh and I wanted to grab it, but I kept my composure. I leaned over the bar and ordered a Corona from the slim, Asian bartender. She was cute as hell, but too small for my taste. I can't fuck a skinny girl; I need something to hold. I would literally break her.

I turned, looked at Jasmine and watched her as I waited on the bartender to pour my beer into a cup. She sipped a red drink out of her plastic cup and laughed as her friends danced and snapchat videos of each other. The bartender tapped my arm and slid my beer over to me.

"It's seven dollars," she said with a smile.

I pulled out some cash from my pocket and gave her a ten-dollar bill. "Keep it." I turned back around and leaned on the bar and took a sip of the beer. I had to say something to her; I wanted to talk to her. Maybe I could get her number, but it starts with a conversation. I waited a minute as she continued to laugh at her friends, but I decided to speak up before she left the area.

I leaned in close to her and asked, "Are you on Snapchat too?" I pointed to her friend who was recording her other friend dance around. She smelled of a sweet vanilla scent.

7

I wanted to lick every part of her body she smelled so good. I literally wanted to pick her up where she stood, prop her onto the bar in front of us and tear her jeans off of her entirely to expose what I just knew had to be the prettiest pussy ever. But I had to be cool; I couldn't do what I really wanted to.

"Of course. I think everyone has it," she laughed.

"I just got on it. You're right, everyone is on it."

She shook her head yes and sipped her drink. She pulled her phone out and opened up her snapchat. "Can you record me?" She handed her phone to me with a smile.

"Yea." I put my beer down and took her phone.

She stepped back and ran her fingers through her hair, fixing it into place. The bright flashlight came on and she performed for the camera. In the quick ten seconds, she seductively danced and twirled around, singing along to the song. She was gorgeous and sexy as hell. I was damn near mesmerized by her shape. I wanted to fuck the shit out of her immediately. I imagined myself picking her up right on the club floor, turning her around and bending her over.

I just needed one chance to give her this dick and have her sprung so hard that every time she was horny, I was the first person to come to her mind. All I needed was one chance and I knew I could have her coming back time and time again. I was confident in my dick. It wasn't the average nigga's dick; it was that king mandingo dick that puts a bitch to sleep right after. It was the type of sex that makes women crazy. So crazy they are cooking you meals, buying you things and stalking your social media to see if you're giving that good dick to anyone else.

I knew that my dick was the kind that could basically have women do anything. I had women fight over me, leave their man for me, and even be a side chick for me, all for the love of this dick. I knew I was blessed and talented and just wanted the chance to give her the blessing of a lifetime.

After I recorded her dancing, she watched it replay and smiled. "Thanks. What is your snap name?"

"It's Fox45," I replied. I pulled my phone out and saw that she followed me, so I followed her back. It was a start. "Aight, well I'm gonna get out ya way. I see you with your girlfriends."

"Ok, see ya, Fox." She waved, smiled and rejoined her friends.

I walked away satisfied. It wasn't a phone number, but it was definitely the new way of sending direct messages or videos. I was going to fuck. She wanted the dick and I could tell. I smirked as I walked back over to my boys, who were sitting in a VIP section. The bouncer stepped to the side and allowed me in.

"Yo', I'm going to fuck Jasmine," I said as I sat down.

"What? You ain't hitting that. She's a good girl," Joey replied in disbelief.

"Yea. She's one of those girls who don't give it to nobody. I'm surprised she is even in this type of club," Rev chimed in.

I leaned back in my seat on the couch, "Y'all don't have no faith?"

"Hell no," they both said in unison and burst out laughing. I just shook my head. I knew what I was capable of and I was already planting the seeds to success. I always win.

The cute waitress walked over and smiled at us. "What are you drinking?" she asked as I dug into my pocket for some money.

"Patron, and give me a Sprite with it," I answered.

"Three hundred dollars." She stood there while she watched me peel off three hundred dollar bills.

"Here," I handed her the money, but grabbed her hand as I put it in. Then I pulled her close to me and got in her ear. Her soft dark brown hair rubbed against my cheek and I reached up to move it away from her ear. "When you gonna stop playing, girl?"

She rolled her eyes and smiled. "I'll be right back with your bottle, Fox."

By the end of the night, me and my team were close to the bottom of the bottle. Kayla, the waitress, came back over to the table to grab any trash and clean up. I shoved a hundred-dollar bill down her corset in the middle of her cleavage. She pulled it out slightly to see what bill it was and smiled graciously at her tip. I always made sure to take care of her when I was there. She was the cutest waitress in there and always took care of me with a section when I came. I knew little about her, but I did know she worked another job during the week and did this on the weekend. She was a little hustler and was only a tender 23.

Once we left the club, I got in my car and pulled my phone out. I sent Jasmine a goodnight message to her snapchat inbox and told her to get home safely. I wasn't playing no games. I was going after that pussy. I checked my other phone and had five missed calls. I knew it was someone wanting some work. I tossed the phone to Joey and it landed in his lap. I was going to let him handle it. I was tired and tipsy and had to focus on driving home. His car was at my house so we went there with no stops and then he went his separate way. I pulled into my driveway and hit the garage door opener and went

10

right in. I could hear my dog barking in the back as usual, as I headed inside my house. I threw my keys on the marble counter top in the kitchen and headed upstairs. I didn't even bother taking my clothes off or changing. I fell directly into bed and by this time, I noticed Jasmine replied to my snap; she simply said goodnight.

The sound of my dog barking woke me out of my sleep and I squinted my eyes, adjusting to the light. My head pounded from the drinking I did last night as I woke up. After rubbing the sleep out of my eyes, I picked up the phone to see it was almost 3 p.m. I couldn't believe I slept so long and now someone was approaching my house. My dog barked more angrily and I looked out the back window to check on him. There was nobody back there; he was safe. Then I looked out the bedroom window to the front of the house and saw a white Lexus I didn't recognize.

"Who the fuck?" I mumbled to myself.

I headed down the steps to the front door, opened it and stood in the doorway, looking as intimidating as I could. I softened up once the car door opened and I saw who emerged from it. Kayla hopped out and closed her door and locked it. She began up the driveway and smiled as she saw me. She had on a pair of burgundy sweat pants with a t-shirt and sneakers on; comfortable and cute.

"Look who it is," I grinned as she approached the doorway.

"Hey, Fox."

"Come in." I stepped aside for her to enter.

"I just wanted to drop this off. You left it last night at the club. I saw your license in it so that's how I found your house. It's beautiful, by the way," she replied as she looked around the outside.

She was surprised at the size and quality of my home, I could tell. She expected me to live somewhere raggedy like the rest of the guys who come to the club and throw their rent money around.

"I didn't even know I left this. Thank you." I reached out and grabbed the wallet. "You can still come in, though."

"I can't stay long." She side eyed me but stepped inside. Immediately, she began admiring the inside of my house as she did the outside. "This really is beautiful."

"Thank you." I led her to the family room. "It's just me here. I need a wife to be here with me to help decorate some more." I eyed her, flirting.

"Cut it out, Fox," she laughed.

"I'm serious. I have everything else I want but a wife. Someone to be here to take care of me. That's all I need. She will have everything I have and more."

"Well, you better get to looking. I'm sure you have all the baddies after you," she teased.

I was never short on ladies at all, and Kayla was well aware of my reputation around town. I was young, handsome, rich and had good dick. The ladies loved it and it was never hard to get them to fall head over heels. I didn't have a girlfriend, or even a main chick at the moment. I have been so busy hustling that I really didn't have the time to focus on a woman. They require way too much time and that is time taken away from my money. So, I just fucked bitches and kept a rotation going. It was simple, carefree, drama free and not time-consuming.

"Well, what you doing for the rest of the day? It looks like you just woke up." She turned her nose up jokingly.

"I did. Too much Patron last night."

"It's after three in the afternoon. Damn!"

"I know what time it is. I'm about to get myself together. I got some business to handle."

"Business? I don't even want to know." She rolled her eyes and stood up. "I'm going to get out of here."

"Wait a second. Why so fast? Chill for a minute with me." I walked over to her and pulled her off the couch, close to me.

"I have things to do. This is the only free time I have when I'm not working."

"It ain't gonna hurt you to spend a little time with me. I know you work a lot. I have to make it up to you anyway for bringing my wallet back."

I pulled her body even closer to mine and slid my hands down to palm her ass. I could tell she liked it because she didn't pull away completely. She was mentally fighting it, but I knew she wanted this dick.

"How you gonna make it up?" she asked curiously.

"Let me show you."

I grabbed her face and tongue kissed her and she melted in my arms. I kissed her neck as I reached up her shirt and caressed her breasts through her bra. I pulled her shirt over her head and pulled her breasts outside of the bra and kissed them. Her nipples began to stand erect for me. I took her bra off while she began to untie her sweat pants. Once she stepped out of them, I took a second to admire her perky young frame. It was curved in all the right places and was just waiting for me to invade it.

13

She dropped to her knees and pulled down my pants and boxers and hungrily fed on my dick. I shoved it in and out of her mouth and watched it disappear into her warm, moist mouth. No feeling is better than forcing your dick down a bitch's throat. I had to slow down because I almost bust in her mouth. I pulled her up and bent her over the sofa and slid inside her vagina. She moaned in pleasure as I slowly built a consistent rhythm inside of her. Switching from position to position, we worked ourselves up and I finally pulled out and bust all over her stomach. I cleaned her up, kissed her forehead and disappeared into my kitchen for some water. She got dressed and was ready to head out when I returned.

"Aight, you kept me here long enough; I told you I have things to do," she joked and walked towards the door.
"Ok, babe. Now, you got the address, so don't be a stranger." I followed her to the door and opened it for her. She turned to hug me goodbye and headed out the door.

"Wait, I still didn't make it up to you." I smiled.

She stopped and turned back to look at me. "You already did," she said confused.

"Just come here," I said.

She walked back over to me and I pulled out some cash from my jean pocket. I counted out five hundred dollars and handed it to her. She smiled a huge grin and kissed me and said thanks. She left happily and more satisfied than when she arrived. As she pulled off, I saw Joey pull up behind her, so I left the door unlocked and drank my water, as I sat on the steps waiting for him.

Joey came inside wearing a pair of sweats, a hoodie and Timbs. He looked like he threw on the first thing he found and

14

was wrinkled. He urgently walked in, uninvited. I knew something was up.

"They shot Rev," Joey blurted out.

"What? Who? He ok?" I was suddenly wide awake.

"I don't know, man. He at the hospital, but they won't let me see him because I'm not family. I don't even know who it was or what happened."

Rev was like my little brother. He grew up around the corner from me and his pops was like the OG in the neighborhood. I looked up to his pops and he taught me a lot of what I know today about the streets. He was murdered when Rev was just 13 and I took Rev under my wing. His mom was heavy into drugs and when Rev's dad got murdered, she went off the deep end. I think she suffered from mental illness also, so Rev spent a lot of time in the streets with me. I treated him like family and always looked out for him. I promised his mom I would always take care of him.

Joey had no answers for me, so I got dressed and hopped in my car to head to the hospital, with Joey behind me. When we arrived, Rev's mom was there, distraught. I ran to her and offered her my comfort, but she pulled away immediately. Confused, I stepped back and tried to figure out why.

"You stay away from me and Rev!" she shouted at me.

"What?" I replied. I didn't understand where this was coming from. I would never stay away from Rev.

"This is all your fault. You have him running your drug deals for you and shit. This is your fault!" she rambled on.

"I would never put Rev in any harm. I love him. That's like my brother," I defended myself.

"You stay away. You got him shot. You did this!" She sobbed and walk off to go to her son's room.

15

I couldn't figure out how she would blame me. I looked out for that nigga like he was my own blood. She knew he sold drugs. Shit, she did drugs and Rev's dad sold drugs when he was here. What the fuck was she blaming me for? I was at a loss for words and in order for the ruthless nigga not to come out of me, I gracefully backed down and left.

I needed to find out what happened and who did it. Not only for Rev's revenge, but for my own safety. I didn't know if it was a personal beef or something my organization needed to worry about. Right now we were thriving, and usually when you're riding a high wave, it's always someone or something that wants to bring you down. It's almost inevitable. It always happens that way. So even though we didn't have any beef with anyone currently, you can never rule out the haters that have been watching, lurking and waiting for the perfect moment to attack.

Rev was real flashy so it could have just been a robbery. People knew he had money and he was not shy about showing it. A luxury Benz sat in his parking spot at his luxury condo. He always had designer clothes on and it was no secret he didn't hesitate to spend money when he was out. You could catch him at the local strip club, throwing out money, or at a 5-star restaurant, eating good. His reputation around the city was well known. I, on the other hand, was a little more low-key with mine. I made more money than Rev, but I was also smarter. I moved out the city to a surrounding neighborhood and rarely let anyone know where I stayed, which is why I was so surprised to see Kayla earlier.

There were endless thoughts running through my mind and I had to sort them out. I told Joey to meet me at the pool hall so we could figure some stuff out. When I got there, my

16

boy Chuck was there, already playing pool with Joey. I went straight to the bar to sit down. My head was spinning because of Rev's situation, but also, all that Patron last night had my stomach feeling crazy.

"Yo' nigga, I been calling you all day. Where the fuck you been?" Chuck said as he dapped me up when I sat down.

"My bad. I was hungover all day. Throwing up and shit," I lied, knowing I was sleeping and fucking all day. I asked the bartender for some water.

"I told you about that drinking shit. Its gonna throw you off your game one day. You can't be MIA like that. This ain't a fucking game." Chuck had a real attitude now hearing my excuse.

"Fuck outta here with that dad shit. I don't ever be off my game. This was one time. Chill out," I spat back. "And Joey had my work phone. Why didn't you hit my other line?"

Chuck leaned down to take his shot at the ball on the pool table. He was winning so far and they had four hundred dollars on the game. He steadied his hand and eyed the ball and the pocket, then went for it. He watched as his shot did exactly what he intended it to do, and proudly stood up straight. "Well, while you were away, nursing your baby hangover, Greg went missing."

"What do you mean went missing?" I questioned.

"Did I stutter? That nigga gone. Missing," Chuck repeated himself.

"I mean, missing? Maybe he just hungover too. Y'all checked his crib?"

"Yea, smart ass. We checked everywhere that nigga supposed to be. His baby mom can't even find him."

17

"His phone ring when you call it, or does it go to voicemail?"

"Voicemail." Chuck and I knew that was a bad sign. "And what is worse is that he came and re-upped yesterday. Double."

"Double? Fuck he double up for?" I was confused now.

"I don't know. This dick head over here gave it to him." Chuck smacked the back of Joey's head.

Fox stood up and walked over to Joey, "Why the fuck you give him double without consulting me or Chuck?"

He nervously stuttered out, "I...I...He asked for it. I don't know."

"If that nigga don't turn up, that's on you. You gonna answer for it," Fox said angrily.

He walked towards the door, "Come on y'all, we gotta find Greg."

"Nigga, I'm in the middle of a game. I got four hundred dollars on it." Chuck copped an attitude.

"Man, fuck that game. In the last twenty-four hours, Greg went missing and Rev got shot and don't nobody know shit and you trying to play a pool game."

Chapter 2

Good Girls like Bad Guys

"My last piece of advice, be aggressive. Do not shy away from opportunity. Do not back down to someone who is pushing you away. Do not back down to anyone! Be aggressive. Find a loophole, another window, a different path, but if you are going after something—whether it be a story, a job, an opportunity—be aggressive. If you want it and believe it, do not back down."

The professor finished his final lecture and began to pack his brown leather briefcase up with the papers that lay on his desk. Jasmine picked up her purse and notebook and headed towards the front of the class. Dodging a few students on the way, she finally made it to him before he slid out the side exit.

"Mr. Ortell, can I have a minute of your time?" she called out to him as she approached.

"Sure. Ms. Sutton, right?"

"Yes, Jasmine Sutton." She stopped at the desk and put her purse down on top. "I'm graduating next week and I was wondering if you knew of any opportunities available for new grads? I've been looking and sending my resume all over daily, but it doesn't hurt to ask around as well."

"You're absolutely right. It never hurts to ask. I'm actually glad you did. Most students come to class to pass, but never take full advantage of the resources we have to offer them."

"Yea, you said be aggressive," she smiled.

"Well, I do know a company that is looking for an on-air host. They are looking to hire immediately and well, to be honest, I think you're the perfect fit for it. Now that this is our last class together, I can say it; you're beautiful. You would do well on air. How are your investigative skills?"

"Thanks! I'm pretty good. I've always had an interest in investigative journalism and broadcast, so this sounds amazing," Jasmine poured with excitement.

"Ok then, here is what I can do for you. Email me over your resume, cover letter and any writing samples or a reel that you have done. I will personally send it over to my contact there. I know they are desperately looking to fill the spot, so you should hear something back quickly."

"Mr. Ortell, I really appreciate this. It means a lot! I will be sending the stuff tonight."

Jasmine wasted no time revising her resume and gathering up her samples and reels and sending them over. She was beyond excited for the opportunity and wanted to tackle it head on. Within three days of submission, she already had an interview lined up. She hadn't even graduated yet, but it was right around the corner. The company took a copy of her transcripts as evidence of graduation, and they fell in love with her upon meeting. She was exactly what they were looking for physically to be on camera, and she had the skill, education and interest in the particular position. Her duties would be to find stories, develop them, research them, fact check, write her hard copy and present them on air nationally.

Her life was about to change drastically within a few days and she was more than ready for it. Her face would be on nightly news segments that broadcast across the country. It was an incredible experience and she worked every day for something like this. They hired her and told her she would start on Monday. As soon as she left the interview, she went shopping for a new on-air wardrobe. They said she would not be provided wardrobe until her six-month probation period was up. Until then, she was on her own and she planned on walking in there and stealing the entire show.

Over the weekend, she practiced her on air sign on and sign off. She wanted to be perfect for the job and there was no better way to perfect it than sitting in front of a mirror, going over lines. She let no distractions in until she got a message on Snapchat from Fox. The smile that formed on her face was an indicator that she was due for a break. She leaned back in her chair and replied quickly to his request for a lunch date.

"Sure, where do you want to go?" she replied.

"Do you eat sushi?" he asked.

"Yea, I do."

"Meet me at 3rd and Market. I know a nice place around there."

"Ok, I'll be there in 45 minutes," she replied.

She put her phone down and stared in the mirror at herself. "What am I doing?" she asked herself as she got up and looked in her closet for something to put on. She hesitated about even going because she knew what type of things Fox was into. He seemed like a street dude and that's not what she wanted. She wasn't sure what he did exactly, but she had an idea. Finally, just deciding to take a break after getting dressed, she grabbed her phone and her purse and headed out to meet him on time.

When she arrived, she frowned at the price of valet for her car, but didn't have the time or patience to drive around, searching for parking. Fox was nowhere to be found, so she took a seat at the bar to wait for him. Regretting that she never exchanged numbers with him, she sent him a snapchat message, letting him know she was there. After finishing her first martini, he replied and said he was parking. Her mind was racing with thoughts about him. She didn't know anything about him, but she knew he was attractive. Being single for the last year has caused her to become sort of a serial dater. Going out with guy after guy and never finding a successful candidate, she was beginning to think her standards were just too high. His lateness was already strike one and his lateness caused her to have to pay for her own valet.

"I'm sorry I'm late," he apologized as soon as he approached her and gave her a light hug.

His eyes immediately went to her wide hips and thighs; she was built naturally curvy. A lot of women were getting work done on their body to get what she had naturally. He took a few seconds just to admire her body. Her waist was tiny and her breasts sat heavy. Her skin tone was almond brown and her complexion was perfect. Her teeth were straight and white; he was impressed. She didn't look like the typical girl from around the neighborhood; she stood out. She looked like she took as much pride in her appearance as he did sitting next to her.

She smiled, "It's ok." Once she got a better look at him in the light and outside of the club atmosphere, she was even more impressed. He dressed nice, looked clean and smelled good. He was fine! She especially loved his chocolate skin. Something about that smooth dark skin was her weakness. His was covered in tattoos, which normally wouldn't be her thing, but it slightly turned her on today. He was so different than what she typically went for. He ordered a Corona and looked over the menu. When he lifted his head, she was smirking at him.

"What?" He low-key blushed at her gaze.

"Nothing. I can't look at you?"

"You have something to say or you just going to look?" he questioned.

"I'm just going to look for now," she flirted.

The bartender returned with Fox's Corona and took their food orders. After a couple more drinks, a little more flirting and their sushi meals, they concluded that there was a mutual interest. Jasmine learned not to rush things with dating. She just wanted to enjoy someone's company before asking 101 questions, which would lead her to lose interest too quickly. Her goal was to not judge and just have a good time. They had a good chemistry and by the end of the date, Jasmine was sure she wanted to see him again.

"Excuse me," Fox said as his phone vibrated in his lap. He picked it up and took the call in private. It didn't bother Jasmine since she just met him; she understood privacy.

"I hate to eat and run, but I gotta get out of here. I have some business to handle. I really hope we can get together again, though." He pulled out money from his pocket and stuffed it in the black holder for the check. The bartender picked it up and disappeared.

"Yeah, I had a good time. We can do it again. Take my number."

"Oh, I passed the test? I can get the number now?" he joked.

"Yea, you passed with a seventy-five percent," she laughed.

"Oh, did you valet?" he asked.

23

"Yea," she answered.

He handed her a twenty-dollar bill and she smiled and thanked him, then they exchanged numbers and Fox hurried out. Jasmine asked for a glass of water before she left. She had three drinks and felt a little bit of a buzz. Luckily, she didn't live far and was home safely in no time. Her roommate was at work so she still had the rest of the day to try to work on her lines in the mirror. She pulled a chair up and sat down in front of the long full body length mirror and admired herself.

"I'm Jasmine Sutton and this is your nightly news. Tune in tomorrow, 6 p.m.," she slurred out and giggled, realizing she was too tipsy to even practice.

Her mind flipped back to her date and she smiled to herself at the thought of Fox. She was excited at the possibilities to come with him. She imagined being so close to him and running her hands up and down his arms, feeling all of his muscle definition, while following his tattoos with her fingers. She thought about kissing him lightly on the lips, opening her mouth, allowing his tongue in while his hands ran down her lower back as he pulled her closer to his body. Eventually, his hands would cuff both of her cheeks and he would grind his pelvis into hers slowly. She could feel his hard dick up against her thigh. The thought of this made her pussy wet.

She began to rub her breasts through her shirt and unbuttoned it to expose them. While she rubbed them, she watched herself in the mirror and began to slowly grind back and forth in her chair. She continued to think of Fox as she stood up and pulled her jeans and shirt off. Left in her bra and panties, she sat back down and rubbed her clit through her panties. She continued to grind back and forth, as her fingers

24

rubbed her clit and she felt the wetness through her panties. Her pointer finger slid under her panties and into her vagina slowly. Gently, she pushed it deep inside of herself as she daydreamed of Fox. In and out, she slowly pushed her finger deep into her vagina and built up a steady rhythm.

Soft, subtle moans escaped her mouth as her rhythm got harder and faster. She imagined Fox's mouth in between her legs, sucking on her juices. The image in the mirror with her legs spread apart was turning her on even more. She slowly put a second finger in and moaned out, while she flicked her two fingers up and down, massaging her spot. In a matter of minutes, she was leaking through her panties and on the chair as she orgasmed. Her moans grew louder and became uncontrollable as her whole body tensed up until she finished. She breathed out heavily and tried to regain her composure. All she wanted to do was sleep next and that's exactly what she did. She pulled off her panties, crawled into her bed and fell into a deep nap.

About an hour later, her roommate, Jess, walked in and woke her. She rolled over and stretched her body out and let her eyes adjust to the light. Not ready to wake up, she sighed and laid there and watched her roommate walk past her room to her own room. In a few minutes, she forced herself to get up and walked over to Jess' room.

"Hey," Jasmine said, still rubbing the sleep out of her eyes.

"Hey girl, what's up?" Jess asked as she looked up from her laptop. She turned down the music playing on her computer.

"So, I met a boy," Jasmine grinned.

"Aw shit." Jess reached up and closed her laptop. "Who?"

Jasmine walked in the room, sat on the bed next to her and got comfortable. She leaned back against the wall, all the while still smiling. She was blushing already and she didn't even start her story about Fox yet. She could hardly contain her excitement. Even as fresh as it was, it was making her smile.

"I just met him, but I really like talking to him. We have a really good vibe."

"That's good! It's always hard to find that."

"Yea. We got a good chemistry. It's very new, but I like him so far."

"Ahhh, how new? Where did you meet him?"

"Just one date. We met at the club." Jasmine covered her face with her hands in shame.

"Damn girl. Give it three weeks, he will be the next fuck boy on the list." Jess laughed.

"No! Don't say that," Jasmine whined.

"I mean come on, they all start good. But you met this nigga in the club, first of all. That is never a good start. How old is he?"

"He's 28."

"Ok, that's not bad. He is older, so maybe he's a little more mature. What does he do?"

Jasmine looked down. "He's a dope boy, I think."

"Girl bye," Jess sucked her teeth. "You already know what I'm going to say. You know I went through some bullshit in my past because of that lifestyle. My ex in jail now and he ain't coming back anytime soon."

"I know, I know. It's not something I would typically consider, but it's not every day I'm actually feeling someone."

"Trust me, it's not worth it. No matter how focused you are on staying out of that business of his, you have no choice but to be involved if you're dating him seriously."

"I mean I don't have to be involved in it; it's not my business, that's his."

"Don't be naïve. Just trust me, shit gets real. It's not a joke. You can really get caught up."

"I'm a big girl, I can handle it. I'm not worried about it. As long as he doesn't do it around me, I'm cool."

"You not hearing me, but you gonna have to learn for yourself, just like I did. I got secrets I'm taking to the grave from being around that shit."

"Secrets?" Jasmine perked up and rubbed her hands together. "Do tell."

"I just said I'm taking them to the grave!" They both laughed.

"Come on, I won't tell anyone. Please."

"Listen, just take my advice. Get out now and not later," Jess advised.

"I'll be careful. Don't worry." Jasmine slid off the bed. "I mean it just started. Let's just see if it even goes anywhere."

She walked off a little disappointed that her friend was so negative about it. Her assumptions that something would go wrong right off the bat pissed her off. It made her feel insecure about the situation for just a moment, but Jasmine was determined to see where it could go with Fox. There was no stopping her when her mind was made up; a stubborn Taurus trait of hers.

Jess never disclosed why her ex-boyfriend was in jail or what happened. Matter of fact, she never spoke about it at all. She kept it all to herself. The most Jasmine ever knew was that he was a hustler and ended up behind bars. It was really hard on Jess and there was a period when he got locked up that she was depressed and withdrawn. She even wanted to move, but Jasmine convinced her to stay.

For two months, Jess was gone and Jasmine couldn't figure out why she wouldn't come back. She told her she went to go stay with family because she needed some fresh air, so to speak. After a while, Jasmine convinced her she needed to just come back and live life. Hiding from your problems wasn't going to solve them, she told her. Eventually, she returned and slowly transitioned into the person she used to be.

As normal as Jess became, she still wouldn't speak about her ex, what he did or why she took it so hard. She went to visit him almost every Sunday, though, and Jasmine just left it at that. As long as her friend was back to being herself, she didn't bother bringing it up and asking questions.

Jasmine went back to her bedroom, got into bed and curled up with her phone. She spent the next hour texting Fox. She giggled and blushed like a young girl, but luckily, no one was around to see her gushing over her new guy. Deep down inside, her friend telling her to stay away from his type made her want him more. As the saying goes, good girls always like bad boys.

Chapter 3

Familiar Face

"Listen, nigga, I know you know something, so to make this a lot easier on you, just tell me, because the longer this goes on, the worse it will be for you. Not for me, because I can do this all night," I said as I smacked the young boy tied to the chair in the face.

"I told you I don't know shit," he whimpered out. "I didn't hear shit, I didn't do shit and I didn't see shit."

"I don't believe you."

"Real talk. Everything been real cool. Real regular around the way. Ain't no beef!"

"It ain't been regular around our way and it's looking like your boss is the reason."

"He ain't mention nothing to me. I swear I don't think he had nothing to do with it," the kid tried to explain.

Joey and Chuck were leaned against the table in the garage, watching. Joey pulled a hit on his blunt and exhaled the smoke as he began to pace back and forth. His mind raced as he thought of the many possibilities of what went wrong. There were still no answers about Rev, and Greg and Joey were convinced this kid knew something.

"Man, fuck that, Fox. That nigga know something," Joey said as he walked up to the guy and shoved his fist in his gut. "Talk muthafucker!"

"Ahhhh, I don't know nothing," he coughed out.

"This nigga lying. Who the fuck shot Rev?" Joey continued to punch the kid in the stomach and a few times in

29

the face. He was spitting out blood from a busted lip and coughing to catch his breath, as Chuck stepped up.

"Aight, yo', chill out," Chuck said. "That's enough."

"Enough? Rev in critical condition. Nigga might die and you talking about that's enough." Joey punched the kid again. "Fuck that."

"I said chill. He ain't talking." Chuck cut in and got in front of Joey.

"You always gotta be the voice of reason. Fuck you care if I beat him the fuck up?" Joey yelled back at Chuck.

"Nah, you gotta chill, Joey." I stepped in this time. "If I find out you lying to us and you or your boss had anything to do with Rev getting shot, or know anything about Greg, it is going to be problems for you. Believe me; I'm a man of my word." I untied the kid's hands and he rubbed his wrist to ease the pain.

I picked my keys up off the table and headed towards the door; Chuck followed behind. Joey grabbed the kid by the arm, yanked him out the seat and pulled him behind us. We left the building and I locked it up behind us. I started my car and waited for them to get inside. Chuck got in the front seat and Joey opened the back door.

"Don't get any blood on my seats either," I said and looked in my rearview mirror. "Matter fact, put him in the back."

Joey opened the trunk of my truck and pushed the kid in. It was an open trunk, so it wasn't too bad. I just didn't want him leaking on my seats, fucking shit up. Joey slammed the trunk shut and got in the back seat. I headed off to drop the kid off in the middle of nowhere, on his own. He would be ok. He could find his way back home by a taxi or some shit. I didn't

30

care; I had shit to do with the rest of my day. After that, I dropped Joey's hyper ass off because me and Chuck had a meeting with our distributors. They heard that Rev had got shot and the rumors of Greg missing. They didn't give a fuck about either one of them and they didn't even know Greg personally, but they knew both of them were a solid part of my team. This meeting was to confirm that their investment was safe and they had nothing to worry about, I assumed. I had to reassure them that business is still planned as usual. I didn't even have assurance myself honestly, but I wasn't about to tell them that. No way was I fucking up the connect I had.

I got linked up with these guys when I did some time. I served nine months for some dumb ass drug charges that eventually got thrown out on some technicality shit. Somehow, the evidence needed went missing. Somehow. I know how, but we will just say somehow. Inside, on my very first day, I got tested by everybody. The white boys checked me, the Spanish boys checked me, even the niggas checked me. I didn't know how I was going to survive in there because on the outside, I was an enemy to all of them. Inside was no different.

I ran into some niggas that used to serve work around my way years ago. We almost had a full out war over some territory, but things died down before they could get too crazy. They backed down when their leader's wife and son got kidnapped. We held them for five long days. The hardest five days of his life where he got a message every day with a threat to kill them if he didn't make his men back off our area. Eventually, he gave in and they found new neighborhoods to occupy, and he took his wife and son back peacefully. He knew retaliation would mean a lot of bloodshed on both ends. The thought of losing his family in a war put things into

31

perspective for them, so he took that loss and moved on gracefully, with respect.

So, walking into the cafeteria on day one and who do you guess I see? This same nigga whose wife and kid we snatched up. He walked past me with the biggest smirk on his face and I knew that only meant one thing: he was coming back to get me and I had to be prepared. The problem is, I was alone on the inside. Day by day, I watched my back and all of my surroundings until I saw something that might help me out. The Spanish boys had beef with the same nigga I was watching out for. I noticed their back and forth argument one day and the way they stared each other down. I had to become cool with the Spanish for protection. That right there would be a challenge itself. I was not Spanish; I was black as hell.

Soon, I got to talking to this young guy about the outside and where he was from. Turns out, he was from around my area and was due to be released in the next month. I told him when he was out, to look for Rev and Chuck and they would be able to get him some work to get money to get back on his feet right away. He was grateful and we began to look out for each other from that day. He was only going to be here for another month, so I urged him to introduce me to his people. Everyone was a bit standoffish at first and didn't trust my intentions. I told them the truth: I hated the niggas they hated and wanted to be around if they ever had to take them down.

Long story short, the Spanish kid I befriended ended up being a blessing in more ways than one. Once he got out and linked up with Chuck, they were doing their thing while I was still locked up. As soon as I returned home, my mind went from 0 to 100; straight business and I wanted to build an empire. I was dead broke and hungry. I had to do something to change my life and get my hands on some money. The Spanish kid knew an older guy who was rumored to have some pretty good connects. One thing led to another and we ended up linking up with this really good connect out in Cali. It was perfect because no one else around here knew about him.

Once our business was up and running, we were bringing in a shit load of money a day. Things really picked up and broke and hungry weren't even in our vocabulary anymore. The Spanish kid was a lot like Joey: a hot head with a quick temper and never thought twice. He never took the time to think before speaking or considered his options before acting. That shit cost him his life one day on the streets and while I was forever grateful for his contributions to my life, I knew it would happen to him. People like that never last long; the streets ate them up.

Once me and Chuck arrived at the meeting, we took a seat across from Marcos, the boss' son. He had on a suit, which was unusual because he was usually dressed down when we saw him. He looked neat and cleaned up; an upgrade from his norm. His hair was even cut low. He used to have long hair that he pulled into a ponytail. It was all gone. He looked like a new man; a grown man.

"My dad couldn't be here today. He has some personal things to take care of, but from now on, you will be dealing with me directly." He smiled.

"Marcos, my man," I reached out and shook his hand. "Looks like someone's stepping up."

"Something like that. I've been around my dad and his business for so long, I know it just as well as he does. It's time

33

I assist him with things and take some of the responsibility off of him."

"Yeah, that sounds right," I replied.

"Well, to make this short and to the point, I wanted to let you guys know that personally, we work very well together and I don't want this transition to change the way we handle things. The only difference is you come to me and not my father."

"Yea, ok, cool. That's good with us," I said and looked to Chuck for confirmation. He shook his head in agreement.

"Cool," Marcos said. "I have also been hearing some rumors. Some things been going on. Is everything ok?"

"Yea. Everything is good," Chuck spoke up.

"What is it that you have been hearing?" I asked. I was curious how things got all the way back to him.

He stood up and buttoned his suit jacket. "Just some things about people being shot and missing. I just want to make sure that my investment is protected at all times. I don't want to get a call that there's some war going on and it's affecting my sales. I still expect my money on time."

Marcos had put on his big boss drawls this morning I could see. He was feeling himself and his new position. I had to respect it. I assured him everything was fine and he would have his money at the usual time and place, with no problems. We left on a positive note and by this time, it was getting late. I did enough shit for the day and just wanted to smoke a blunt and get some pussy.

My mind immediately went to Jasmine, but I knew she wasn't fucking this fast. I knew I was going to have to put in work for hers, so I called Kayla and told her to meet me at my crib. Of course, she was going to come hungry for this dick and some more cash, but after waiting at home for thirty minutes, I got a call from her saying she couldn't get a babysitter. I was pissed. Fuck her young ass doing with a baby already anyway.

I decided to try my luck with Jasmine. I called her and it took a little convincing, but after a short while, I got her to agree to come over and watch a movie. I needed this chill time to get my mind off Rev and Greg. I was internally driving myself crazy trying to figure out what happened to them and was constantly worrying about how Rev was doing in the hospital.

When Jasmine arrived, I let her in and she walked in looking beautiful as ever. She was amazing and when I say amazing, I really mean it. I don't usually get sprung off a woman, but I would literally do anything she asked me, just so I could fuck her. She had on black tights and a t-shirt with Biggie and 2pac on it. She looked real cute and comfortable. She slid her Jordan's off and sat on the couch next to me. I just stared at her and she started blushing.

"Here you go again. Boy, what are you looking at?" she smiled.

"You, Jazz."

"Jazz? Oh, that's cute." She leaned back on the couch.

"Yea, can I call you Jazz, or would you prefer something else? Bae? Wifey? Boo boo kitty?"

She laughed at the nicknames and agreed that Jazz was fine. We found a movie on Netflix and got comfortable with each other. She leaned back on me and I asked her how her day was. She talked on and on about this job she's about to start and I could tell she was excited. She went into a lot of detail about it and the enthusiasm in her voice gave it away. Shorty was dope. She had a lot going on and it was shit I wasn't used to dealing with. She had what a lot of these bum bitches that I met didn't have. It was sort of stuck up in a way, but she was so damn beautiful I didn't care if she thought she was better than the next bitch because she was.

This girl has never been around a street nigga a day in her life; I could tell. I knew I would be able to mind fuck her as well as fuck her soon enough. This was going to be like taking candy from a baby. She wasn't stupid or anything—the girl had her life together—but she wasn't street smart. I wasn't surprised. I had a plan for her, though.

After she told me about her day, I started to tell her about mine. I wanted her to know the stress I was going through to give her an idea of what my life was like. She listened intently. I think the bad boy image turned her on, so I played into it as much as possible. She wanted a street nigga; good girls always do.

"I gotta figure this shit out. Rev getting shot is really fucking with me because that's my young boy. I need him to pull through and tell me what happened."

"Damn, that's crazy. And no one has told you if he's even awake or how bad he's hurt?" she asked.

"No, because his mom wouldn't let anyone in the damn hospital room, but I'm hearing a little bit of shit on the streets. He supposed to be in a coma, I heard."

"I wonder if the police have any leads."

"Yea, I haven't heard anything about that either."

"Then, Greg is gone. I don't know what the fuck going on. I don't know if the two are related incidents or what. I can't have these types of problems. To be real, I need both them niggas. We have a system that works for us, now we gotta switch stuff up. On top of that, we gotta have our guard up on 100."

"Yeah, you gotta be careful. You don't want nothing like that to happen to you." She leaned in and kissed me on the forehead.

"I think I got an idea of who did it. We always have problems with them, but it's just little shit; we try to stay out of each other's way. I heard they ain't making money like they used to, though. Could be them trying to start some shit. I just gotta find out if they are responsible."

"Well, you be careful. That's all I can say."

"You want to be my bodyguard?"

She giggled, then her phone rang and she dug in her purse to check it. She ignored it and so did I. Halfway through the movie, I pulled her face close to mine and kissed her, soft then passionately, twirling my tongue against hers. She even tasted good; I just had to have this girl. I began to run my hands across her body and she didn't stop me. I slowly grabbed her breasts and lightly squeezed them. I could tell she was getting turned on, and so was I. Then her phone rang again. She reached back to grab her phone, looked at it and exhaled heavily.

"Let me take this. I'm going to step in the other room." She looked at me disappointedly and got up.

I couldn't hear what was said, but she was gone for just a minute or so. When she returned, I could tell she wasn't happy. She stood towering over me as I sat on the couch with a hard dick and a sparkle of hope in my eye that slowly faded. I knew this bitch was about to leave.

"I gotta go. Something came up," she said sadly.

"Damn, ok. Is everything ok?" I asked with fake concern.

"Yea it is, but I have to take care of something. I'm sorry." She began to put her sneakers on and then grabbed her purse and I got up to walk her out.

"No pressure," I said and headed towards the front door. I shut it behind her. "Fuck!" I said to myself out loud.

I was so pissed off I didn't even bother trying to call Kayla up or anyone else. I took that shit as a loss and took my ass to bed. I turned my phone on silent and went right to sleep. I was not in the mood to handle anyone's shit or talk any business. I did send Jasmine a text before I passed out saying I hoped everything was cool, and we arranged to go out tomorrow to get drinks.

I was really trying to put my time and effort into getting this girl. At first, it was just a fuck I was after, but once I actually talked to her and spent some time with her, I was intrigued. She was the type of woman I should have been going after all along, not the ratchet birds from my past. Those girls were only good for a handful of things, and taking them seriously wasn't one of them.

Jasmine came to my house at 11:30 p.m. and we headed to a hookah lounge called B-Side. We got a table and ordered the mint flavored hookah and waited for the waitress to return to take our drink orders. We decided on getting a bottle because she mentioned one of her friends might be stopping by, so I wanted enough for us all. The waitress brought out a bottle of Cîroc Apple with Ginger ale and cranberry juice. We did the first round of shots and we were all over each other already. My hands ran across her hips and pulled her closer to me in the booth. She slowly ran her hand up and down my leg and knee.

38

We rubbed each other's hands and interlocked fingers. It was quickly starting to look like a relationship. A couple. Boyfriend and girlfriend. There was no denying the chemistry we were developing so early on. I fuck with her.

I got up to go to the bathroom and when I was walking back to the table, I saw someone standing in front of my table. I thought it was Jasmine's friend that was supposed to meet her at first, but the closer I got, I realized there were just guys and no women. Of course, my aggressive, protective nature kicked in.

"What's up?" I asked as I approached the table.

To my surprise, I knew exactly who it was and it sent me from 0 to 100. Jasmine could see the anger in my face and the tension between us immediately. She reached out and grabbed my hand and tried to pull me down next to her, but I was not ready to sit.

"Aye, Fox. What's up? I was just admiring this beautiful girl. This must be you?" The kid smiled.

"Yea, it is. You can go admire something or someone else," I said and took a step closer to him. I tapped my waistband to let him know I was not playing any games. Just a warning to get a nigga out my personal space, especially this kid. I scanned the room to see if I saw any of his boys here that could cause a problem, but saw no one familiar. I was not in the mood for this shit tonight, not while I was out with shorty.

He took two steps back and threw his hands up in surrender, "You got it, Boss."   The kid turned around and walked away through the crowd, back to where he came from. I took my seat next to Jasmine and she was staring angrily at me. I knew she was pissed because the vein in her forehead was popping out. I tried to lean in and kiss on her to relax her, but she pulled away.

"You have a gun on you?" she asked.

"Yea...It's protection, relax."

"Threatening a guy who tried to talk to me with one is not protection. That's intimidation. I don't like that, Fox."

"It's all good. He left," I assured her.

"I don't like that shit," she complained again.

"Well, I don't like it either, but I'm a lot of people's enemy. I never leave home without it."

I decided to try to ease her mind and get her relaxed enough to enjoy the rest of her night, so I poured us both another shot of Cîroc. We threw them back and within minutes, she perked back up and let the liquor guide her to a better place. Her eyes began to get glossy and her movements looser. Cîroc was flowing through her body and she was feeling it. She grabbed my face, turned it to hers and kissed me. This time, she tasted like apple.

Before I could pull back and open my eyes, I heard the all too familiar sound of a gunshot. My first instinct was to duck down below the table and I pulled Jasmine down with me. I just knew in my gut it was intended for me, so I moved quickly. With Jasmine in my left hand and my gun in my right hand, I ran out towards the door. I pushed everyone out of our way with no regard for anyone else's safety. I had to get out, and fast. With all the commotion going on, I didn't even see where the shot was coming from. The crowd, Jasmine and I spilled outside onto the sidewalk and streets, when we heard a second and third shot. This time, my eyes narrowed in on a shooter. It was the kid at my table earlier. The same kid we grabbed and roughed up for information the other day. I knew it was him. We should have offed this kid when we had him tied up.

I raised my right arm and aimed my piece his way and shot two shots. Jasmine was terrified at this point. I held her arm tightly and led the way, while we ran back to my car that was parked around the corner. I lost him from my sight, but I didn't hear any more shots, so I was hoping we lost them. I turned back around and still didn't see anyone following, so I slowed our run to a fast walk. I caught my breath and looked over at Jasmine. Her face was covered in tears and her chest was heaving up and down, as she inhaled and exhaled deeply. When we got to my car, I let her hand go and dug in my pocket for the key.

"Fox, I'm not getting in the car with you! They are shooting at you!" she screamed and backed up from the car.

"Jazz, get in the car! I ain't leaving you out here with these crazy niggas running around."

"I ain't getting in the car. I don't want to get shot!" she yelled at me.

"Jazz, I'm not playing. Get in, we have to get out of here now."

"Leave me alone," she said and started walking down the sidewalk.

"Are you fucking kidding right now? You about to get us both killed. Get in the fucking car." I was starting to get mad.

I got in my car and started to follow her down the street. I rolled down the passenger window and yelled at her again. "Come on, I'm not leaving you out here."

"Get away from me, Fox. They are shooting at you! I'm not trying to be in the car with you when they come back to kill you!"

"You tripping. They shooting because of you. What the fuck you think, they not going to hurt you? You safer with me than without. I'm not going to let nothing happen to you."

She got to the corner and ran across the street, but I got stuck at the red light. I was furious at this point. I needed to get out of this area and here I am, driving slowly behind this bitch who wants to play stupid. I couldn't leave her out here, though; I felt responsible for her and wanted to protect her. I saw a red Honda Civic turn the corner and begin to go down the street she was walking on. I strained my eyes to make out who was in the car, but it was too far. "Oh shit," I said to myself as I prepared to just run the light. I looked both ways, but there were cars still coming. I saw the Honda pull up to her and she stopped walking. It looked like she was talking to them. I gripped my gun tighter, getting ready to use it if necessary. The light changed and I slammed my foot on the gas, shooting myself across the street, closer to them. She opened the back door of the car and looked up and saw me coming. With no hesitation, she quickly got into the car.

What the fuck was going on? Another car pulled out from around the corner behind them and blocked my view as I got closer. I followed them down four blocks and the car made a left turn, so I followed behind. When there was more space, I sped up to the driver side of the car and saw the unexpected; it was a girl. I looked into the passenger side and it was another girl. Jasmine was in the back seat screaming, "Leave me alone! Go home!"

"Pull over yo'!" I shouted to the car while trying to drive. They wouldn't listen to me and continued straight. My natural reaction to get what I wanted was to pull my gun out on them to get them to pull over, but that would just scare her even more. I picked up my phone and called her phone and surprisingly, she answered.

"Yo', who car you in?" I asked out of concern at this point. I didn't care if she got in my car anymore, but I just wanted her safe.

"My friend. Remember I said she was meeting me up there? Just leave me alone. I don't want to talk to you."

"Aight, man." I hung up, annoyed. I was not in the business of begging bitches to talk to me. As long as she was safe with friends, I was getting the fuck out of there. I sped off and went home.

Chapter 4

Trying to Win Her

For the next week, Jasmine wouldn't answer my calls. I was sick. I knew I fucked up, but I didn't think she would really stop talking to me over it. I can't control if someone shoots at me; of course, I'm going to shoot back. She should understand that, I thought to myself. Who wouldn't? Jasmine. She wouldn't even answer my phone calls or return a text. I actually missed her and I don't know how. It was so new, but I actually missed her. I was really starting to feel her.

I couldn't even try to drop in on her because I didn't know her address. The times we went out, she met me out or came to my house first. I was mad as fuck I never insisted on going to her house or picking her up. I didn't know any of her friends, nor had I met any for that matter. I got frustrated just thinking about the fact that I might have lost her for good.

I sat in my bed, thinking of where I could run into her. I could try the club again, but what's the chances of that? Then I remembered she told me she got this new job and she mentioned the name of it. I got to googling it and found the address. I knew exactly what I had to do. I knew she would never expect to see me at her job.

I got out of bed and got dressed and headed out. On the way there, Joey called me talking his usual nonsense. He was nonstop since the shooting. He wanted to find the kid who did it and kill him. I tried to talk him out of it because we don't need the added heat right now. Fuck that young boy. But, Joey was hyped and trained to go. The moment he found out he was shooting at me, he was already locked and loaded, ready to go find the kid. I told him to hold on and wait until we figured things out with Greg and Rev first. One thing at a time.

Once I got to her job, I parked and went to the front door. It was locked and the only way to access it was with a badge. I rang the buzzer and waited. I looked around and felt uncomfortable in this fancy, uppity environment I was in. When the receptionist opened the door slightly, she allowed me inside.

"Hi, can I help you?" she asked and stood in my way.

"Yeah, um…I am looking for someone. Her name is Jasmine," I replied.

She eyed me closely and I knew in her head she was thinking I was up to no good. I didn't look like I belonged there. I looked like a hustler. A street hustler. And that is exactly what I was. She looked at me in confusion.

"Jasmine? Does Jasmine have a last name? A department?"

"I don't know her last name. I know she a journalist."

"Well sir, most of the employees are journalist. You will have to call her and have her come down." She walked back to her front desk and took a seat.

I sucked my teeth, knowing that if I called her, she wouldn't answer. I sent her a text and told her I was at her job, hoping that would make her come down. I waited five minutes and still no reply. The receptionist peeked over at me every couple of minutes with a watchful eye. I wanted to smack her ass across the face for staring at me. She was pissing me off. I called Jasmine and of course, no answer. I waited a few more minutes, hoping she would call back.

The door opened and there stood Jasmine. As corny as it sounds, my heart skipped a beat when I saw her. She stood there looking mean as ever in an all-black dress with an olive green sweater over it. I jumped to my feet, but hesitated. I have been trying to talk to her for so long that now that I had her in front of my face, I couldn't even find the right words.

"Jazz, can I talk to you for a minute?" I took a few steps forward.

"Seriously? I'm at work, Fox." She rolled her eyes.

"Yea, but I just need to talk to you. I'm sorry about what happened. I get that you're mad at me and I want you to know that it will never happen again. I will never bring you around that type of stuff again."

"I can't have this conversation here. I have to go."

"Can you call me later? When you get off?" I pleaded.

"I don't know. I gotta go." She walked back out through the door and disappeared up the stairs.

I didn't feel like I made any progress. I was pissed off at her for making me beg like a sucker. I never did this shit before and didn't know how to feel about it. I was a mixture of mad and hurt. I wasn't used to actually catching feelings for someone and giving a fuck. The way I was acting was out of line, though. Showing up at her job was not even me. I felt like a real sucker nigga. Still, the next few days, I called and still got no answer from Jasmine. I kept calling and texting and was getting no reply.

I spent the next three days sending her flowers and edible arrangements to her job. I didn't call, text or show up again; I just sent her flowers with messages that let her know I missed her and would do anything to make it right. I just wanted to get passed this and move on. On the fourth day, I

46

sent flowers, but got a message from the florist that they were returned. I felt defeated and decided to give up. I can't keep chasing this bitch. I said sorry a million times and she was not trying to hear it. Sometimes you just gotta take a loss. "Fuck it," I said to myself.

In the meantime, I still had my ear to the street trying to find out what happened to Rev and Greg. I was coming up with no leads. I kept hearing that Rev wasn't doing good and was still in a coma. I decided to try to talk to his mom again. I had no choice but to shoot my shot with her and hope I could get her to speak with me. Plus, she had some time to calm down and think rationally.

When I got to her house, I pulled up and parked. I sat in the car for a few minutes, trying to think of what to say or how I should approach this situation. I was so in the dark with what happened that I didn't even know what to say. I walked up to the door and knocked lightly. I waited, but heard nothing. I saw her car sitting out front, so I knew she was home. Rev's car also sat in front of hers. I stared at it for a minute and considered just leaving, but then I heard the locks being opened. The door crept open just enough for a pair of eyes to peek outside and see me. I could barely see who it was, but I saw feminine features, so I assumed it was Rev's mom.

"Hey. Um, can I talk to you for a second?" I rolled my eyes in my head, listening to myself beg another bitch to talk to them.

"Fox, what do you want?" she said through the small crack in the door.

"Can I come in?"

"No."

"I mean I ain't trying to talk through the door, forreal."

47

"What do you want?" she asked again.

"I'm just trying to find out what happened to Rev and find out how he doing."

"He is not good. My baby might die. First, his father, and now him. He gonna die, Fox."

"Damn. I'm sorry. I really am. I want to find the piece of shit who did this to him."

"Why? It should have been you. You should be in his place right now." She sniffled through her tears.

I had to catch myself because I almost said something smart. "Look, I would never want this to happen to him."

"It should have been you!" she raised her voice and slammed the door shut.

I stood still and didn't want to walk away. She was pissing me the fuck off, but I still had no answers and still had no clue what happened to him. I knocked again; I had to get some answers. I know she knew something, but she wasn't telling me. Why would it be me? I never made Rev do anything he didn't already have his mind set to do. He wanted to be a hustler since I've known him. He wanted to be just like his daddy. Unfortunately, he seemed to have the same sad fate as him.

This time, she didn't answer the door, so I walked back down to my car. First, I walked over to Rev's Benz and tried to look through the windows, looking for anything to give me a clue as to what happened, but I saw nothing at all. In even more disappointment, I headed back to my car and left. My mood was shot for the day and there was nothing left to do.

I called Kayla up because if there was anything that would make me feel better, it would be some good, young, tight pussy. She met me up at the bar and we had a couple drinks and caught up. She was a cutie, but didn't have shit going for herself. I chalked it up to her age and that was cool. She just didn't have anything to offer me other than her body. I knew she liked me, but I didn't like her. Not the way I started to like Jasmine. After two drinks, we ordered a third round and a basket of wings.

I turned my head and saw what I did not expect to see and my stomach sunk instantly. Jasmine walked in with her girlfriends and started walking towards the tables behind the bar. Our eyes locked as soon as she walked in. I couldn't hide or even try to act like I didn't see her. When she finally looked away, she looked directly at Kayla and then back to her girlfriends. "Fuck," I said to myself.

"What's wrong?" Kayla asked.

"Oh, nothing. I was just thinking about something I forgot to do today," I lied.

I looked back and saw Jasmine take a seat at her table and she couldn't help but look back up at me. We locked eyes again but this time, she quickly rolled them. When I say she rolled her eyes, she rolled her entire neck and head with them. Great, this was just what I needed, I thought to myself. I turned back to look at Kayla and was disgusted with myself for even being out with her. She rambled on and on about some petty bullshit at the club she works at and I ignored half of it, while throwing in oh yea, right, and true comments here and there.

After I saw the waitress serve drinks and food to Jasmine and her girlfriends, I decided to go say something to Jasmine. I didn't want to just leave Kayla sitting there at the bar alone, but I had to speak. I couldn't see her out and not say anything to her. Kayla leaned over and kissed me on the neck. I leaned back a little, but the deed was done. I was hoping Jasmine wasn't watching. Kayla was starting to feel her liquor and was becoming more and more publicly affectionate. I was ready to leave, but first, I had to say hi.

"I'll be right back. Give me a second," I told Kayla and headed back to Jasmine's table. I stopped in front of it and she and her girlfriends looked up at me inquisitively.

"Hey, Jasmine," I smiled.

"Hey," she said flatly.

"How you been?" I made small talk.

"I'm good. You?"

"Not so good, but I'm cool. Ya know?"

Kayla walked up and stood next to me and said nothing. My nerves got tense and now it was definitely time for the exit. Jasmine frowned her face up at her and I knew it was about to go down. I prayed that I got out of there without any drama.

"Aight, well, I just wanted to say wassup." I started my exit strategy.

"Hi," Kayla said to the table of girls with a slight attitude.

"Hello," the three girls replied almost in unison.

"I'm Kayla," she introduced herself.

"Ok," Jasmine said, returning the same attitude.

"Oh, you don't have a name?" Kayla inquired.

"I do," Jasmine replied with a blank face.

"What's her problem?" Kayla turned to me.

"She doesn't have…" I started to say.

"Excuse me? I'm sitting right here if you want to ask me what my problem is." Jasmine stood up.

"Oh, I see you, but since you don't have a name, I won't address you any further. Like I said, FOX, what is her problem?" Kayla replied and turned back to me.

"Yo' chill out," I told her.

"Chill out? I didn't do shit; she's the one with the attitude," Kayla snapped back at me.

"Bitch, go head from in front of my table with this shit," Jasmine butted in.

"Bitch, I don't have to go nowhere."

"Yo', didn't I just tell you to chill out? I ain't about to do this shit. I'm out," I said and walked towards the door.

Kayla turned to follow and I told her she wasn't riding with me, loud enough for Jasmine to hear. I wasn't about to bring this disrespectful little bitch back with me in front of her. She stopped dead in her tracks when I said that, then continued to walk behind me.

"I'm serious. Get an Uber." I pushed the bar's door open and headed to my car. Pissed was an understatement.

I needed to hit a blunt, so I stopped by Joey's house and rolled up one with him. I told him about what happened and smoked and felt ten times better. Joey just clowned me for being sprung the whole night, but it was all good. I got some good laughs in at my own expense.

When I pulled up to my house, I saw a car parked out front. I wasn't expecting anyone and the closer I got, I realized exactly who it was. I sped up the driveway, hopped out the car and headed down to it. She stepped out the car and slowly walked towards me.

"What's up, Jasmine?" I asked with a huge smile.

"I just thought maybe we could do that talking now," she said and looked down at her feet.

I grabbed her hand and walked with her up the driveway, heading inside my house. I was surprised to see her because I thought that Kayla thing fucked us up for good. We got inside and she slid her heels off and followed me into the family room. She fell on the couch next to me and just stared at me. The same stare I missed so much.

"Now you want to talk?" I questioned.

"Who was that bitch?" she asked.

"A nobody," I replied.

"She had to be someone if you were out with her."

"You see how I left her ass right there, right? She is a nobody."

"Ok fine, you did. Do you promise me you won't ever have me in harm's way again?"

"Of course. I promise. I will let you go your own way if I ever have you around some dumb shit like that again."

She smiled. "Ok."

I had a feeling her seeing me with another girl made her realize how much she missed me too. In a crazy way, I was thankful for the Kayla debacle at the bar. That bitch got me my baby back and some pussy. I fucked the shit out of Jasmine that night. She was everything I thought she would be and I didn't fuck her like I fuck anyone else. I think we made love. I don't know much about that mushy shit, but what we did was not just sex.

Even after it, we laid in each other's arms and just talked. We talked more about her dreams and goals. The topics changed so many times and the conversation just flowed. We were up all night pillow talking. I told her a lot of stuff I normally don't share with anyone else. She made it easy to open up and I was comfortable with her.

"So let me ask you something?" she rolled over to face me.

"Anything."

"What got you into selling drugs? What are your goals? Do you want to just do this forever?"

I hesitated. "Growing up how I did it was all just part of the plan. Most people start working in their parent's company or store or something like that; my family business was drugs. It's all I knew and all I was around, so for me it was normal to start doing it. I started young and learned the game early. Eventually, it got bigger than I ever thought it would be. I never expect to make the money I'm making doing this. It was just a hustle for me in the beginning, but I got to a level where my life changed. I made 1.5 million dollars last year. Ain't no walking away now. I'm in too deep."

"Wow, 1.5? That's crazy. What do you do with all that money? You don't even look like you have that." She laughed.

"I'm smart. I don't want to draw the wrong attention to me. Being flashy is what gets niggas killed or locked up. It's a game of strategy too, but a lot of people fail to practice that part. They just sell, spend and get robbed or locked up. I don't put my money in banks either. That's obviously the common sense part of it. That kind of money with no paper trail is the number one no-no. I got stash spots all over the city. No one knows where except me and my boys. No one knows them all."

"Damn. That's crazy. I hope you're careful. I would be paranoid someone would rob me."

"Yeah, it's risky, but if you trust your circle, then you don't have nothing to worry about. I trust mine 100%."

We fell asleep shortly after that conversation, wrapped up in each other's arms and the blanket. She woke up early and when I opened my eyes, she was already up putting her clothes back on. I laid there and watched her pull up her jeans and zip them shut, then finish with the button. She looked over at me and smiled when she realized I was awake and watching her.

"Good morning," her soft voice said.

"Morning." I rubbed the sleep out of my eye and reached over to grab my cell phone. I looked over the missed calls and text and didn't see anything that needed my immediate attention, so I turned back to her.

"You rushing out of here?" I asked.

"Yeah, I figured I go home and get some stuff done."

"You don't want to go get breakfast?"

She walked over to me once fully dressed, grabbed her cell phone off the nightstand, leaned down to kiss me on the forehead and told me next time. I was disappointed, but shorty had to go. I got up and walked her to the front door and watched her walk out to her car before I closed my door. As soon as I shut the door, my phone rang.

"Yo', nigga. We need to have a meeting asap," Chuck said as I answered.

"Everything cool?" I asked as I put my sneakers on.

"I been hearing some shit. I just wanna see what you think. Meet me at the A spot, now."

"Ok, I'm walking out the door now." I hung up and grabbed my keys.

I figured it was something worth walking right out the door for because he sounded like it was urgent. If he heard any news on Rev or Greg, that was definitely the only thing I was looking forward to hearing. On my way there, I noticed a familiar car behind me a few cars back. I checked my rearview every time I went to turn and they turned too. It was Jasmine's

54

car. I pulled up to the A spot and hopped out. Chuck was waiting out front and saw me pull up. He hopped out his car as well and began to walk towards me.

Jasmine hopped out her car last. "Fox!" she yelled as she began to walk towards me.

Chuck saw her and immediately put his hand on his gun in his waistband, ready to pull it out. I saw his reaction and knew why without words. This was one of our stash spots that no one knew about. I was just as confused as him as to why she was here. I held up my hand to tell him to chill and walked over to her.

"What's good, why you following me?" I questioned defensively.

"I left my charger at your house and my phone died. I couldn't call you."

"How you know how to find me?"

"I mean I saw your car at the light and just followed you. Is that ok?" She sensed the attitude I had.

"Naw. Don't follow me again. It ain't safe for you to be places that I don't know you're going to be. My man was about to pull his gun out because he doesn't know you or what you're doing here. Remember I said I have places that no one knows about. This is one," I explained.

"Ohhh, I'm sorry, Fox. I can just get it later then, my bad," she apologized.

"Nah, I'll just take you back now to get it. Ya phone is dead. Hold up, let me let him know."

"Ok." She walked back to the car and got inside.

"Yo', Chuck, I gotta run past my house real quick. I'll be back in fifteen minutes!" I yelled over to him. He nodded his head and went inside.

The Hyatt Hotel

"So, we can't go back and visit anyone?" Chelsea asked while tears welled up in her eyes.

"No, you can't. It's too risky. We can arrange for Greg to see his parents once a year at a meeting place we set up and arrange. However, we can't make arrangements for you. If you do go back or make arrangements for a visit, you may compromise the whole situation. And because you're not married, we only have an obligation to Greg."

"Right, but married or not, I'm going with him. There can't be any consideration to me as well?"

"No. We already bent the rules to allow you to go with him. Normally, it is only for wives or children. You are just a girlfriend," the detective answered.

"See!" Chelsea shouted at Greg and smacked his arm. "We should have gotten married when I brought it up before." She stood quickly and walked over to the window and began to cry. Greg followed her and wrapped his arms around her shoulders.

"I know baby. I know. We didn't know things would turn out like this."

"So we will have your car downstairs at 4:30. You've got a red eye flight tonight. Once you land, there will be agents who will escort you to your new place. Once things get settled over here and we begin the trial, you will start to hear from us about when you'll have to testify. It's a very smooth process and we will be in touch every step of the way."

"This is fucked up, man. Oregon. What the fuck we gonna do in Oregon?" Greg complained.

"Well, you can always stay here in Philly and take a chance at your own trial for drug trafficking and risk serving twenty plus years, leaving your girlfriend here to raise your unborn son alone. We gave you that choice. You picked this one, not us. Do remember that," the agent said and stood up. "You have until 4:30 to change your mind, but once you get in the car and head to the airport, there is no turning back. This is what happens when you sell drugs. This is what you choose to do and you got caught. Plain and simple."

Greg sucked his teeth and held his girlfriend tighter as she cried even harder. There was no other choice; nothing else to do. He was about to betray his best friend to save himself, but was he really being saved? Oregon was a whole new lifestyle and he hated the idea of it. At least he would be able to raise his son. He told himself that over and over in order to make himself feel ok with his decision.

The agent pulled up to the hotel and sat in the valet spot at 4:25; on time and ready to take Greg and his girlfriend to the airport. They had a private plane waiting for them to head to Oregon. He looked around at his surroundings, then back to the clock; 4:26. The valet guy came over and he rolled his window down to flash his badge.

"Police duty," the agent spoke sternly to the valet attendant.

There was a family of four who pulled up behind him and the attendant jogged back to the driver's side door and reached to open it. The two kids hopped out and bounced around like balls of energy, as the wife got out and walked to the trunk and pulled out two small book bags and handed them to the kids. The husband handed the attendant some cash and went to the trunk to retrieve the rest of the luggage. The agent watched it all in his rearview mirror to pass the time and followed them with his eyes until they walked up to the automatic door in the front of the hotel. The father was stuffing his wallet back in his pants pocket, struggling to carry the luggage and a light jacket at the same time. The wife had nothing in her hands, but she yelled at her kids to follow them because they were running all around the front of the hotel, touching any and everything they could. When they got to the door, Greg and his girlfriend exited and the man with his hands full and head down accidentally bumped into him.

"Oh, my bad," Greg said and helped him pick up his stuff.

"No, that was my fault. I wasn't paying attention."

"All good," Greg replied and handed him his wallet that never made it into his pants and one of his suitcase handles.

The man thanked him and kept walking into the hotel, while Greg made his way to the agent's car. He helped his pregnant girlfriend into the car and got in after her. He closed the door and stared out the window, realizing this was the last and only time he would be able to come back to Philly, his hometown, his life, his family and his friends. The agent glanced back at the clock; 4:30 on the dot.

*   *

I sat on the edge of my bed and looked back at Jasmine sleeping. She had one leg under the sheet and one leg on top of it, curled up to her chest. Comfortable and peaceful, she laid there and I watched her for at least five minutes. Her soft hair

58

was a mess all over her pillow and her makeup from last night was half smeared all over her face, but she still looked beautiful.

My cell started ringing and woke her up, even though I answered it quickly. She stretched and rolled over and pulled the sheet over her entire body, her leg no longer exposed. I pulled up the light blanket at her feet over to her chest. I had a quick conversation with Joey and then got in the shower and got dressed. When I walked out the bathroom, Jasmine was sitting up in bed, on her phone. She looked up and smiled at me.

"Where are you going today?" she questioned and got out the bed to gather her clothes that lay at the foot of the bed in a pile.

"I'm taking you shopping."

"Me? What for?" she asked surprised.

"Just because. Why not?"

"Oh thank you, babe!" She blushed and started putting her clothes on.

When we arrived at the King of Prussia Mall, she didn't know what stores to go in. I think she was being modest, but I told her to get what she wanted and the price didn't matter. She finally loosened up and we started to get item after item. Her hands were full of bags and so were mine.

"You think you got enough?" I joked.

"I don't know. I could get another pair of shoes, of course." She laughed.

"No more shoes. What you get, five pairs?"

"Yup," she said and grinned.

It was getting late, so we grabbed dinner at the food court and headed back to my place. Her car was there, but I

59

didn't want her to leave; I wanted her home to be my home. I had more than enough space for her to move in and we spent all our free time together now anyway. It only made sense. When we pulled into the driveway and got out, I helped her carry all her bags and put them into her car. I wrapped my arms around her to hug her, as she leaned against the driver's side door. I leaned back and kissed her.

"I don't want you to leave," I whined.

"Babe, I been here two days straight. I gotta go home anyway and get new clothes."

"You should just get all of them."

"All?"

"Yea. All your clothes and stuff. Move in."

"Whoa." She stared me in my eyes. "Forreal?"

"Yea forreal. Move in. You don't have to pay for anything. Save your money. All you gotta do is be there and look sexy. Cook occasionally and ya know...clean."

"Um, I haven't even thought about this. That's a big step."

"It is, so think about it. Go home and talk to your roommate. Make sure she's ok with it and let me know. I'll help you move your stuff over."

I knew she had a roommate, but I didn't know anything about her and we still haven't met. Jasmine didn't tell me much about her, just that she had one. I reminded her that if her roommate had an issue financially, then I would pay her half for six months, or less if she found a replacement sooner. I just wanted to end my nights with her every night.

"Ok, I'll talk to her," she replied and kissed me.

Chapter 5

Stash Spot

As soon as Jasmine walked in the house with a handful of bags, Jess enviously eyed her and sat up from the slump she was in on the couch. Jasmine struggled to get them all through the front door, but once she did, she dropped them once she got in and closed the door. Jess completely ignored the phone call she was on and stared in shock at not only the amount of shopping bags, but the types. Luis Vuitton, Gucci, Nordstrom, Louboutin, Saks 5th Avenue and much more.

"Excuse me! When did you hit the lottery?" Jess questioned.

"When I met bae," Jasmine smiled. "Girl, he took me shopping today."

"Clearly. I see." She walked over to the bags and began to look through them. "Oh shit, my bad. I'm going to call you right back." Jess hung her cell up and continued going through the bags.

"He's so great," Jasmine bragged.

"Yeah, until his ass gets locked up. See how great that feels," Jess reminded her.

"Maybe he won't."

Jess stopped and looked up at me. "Girl, they all do. Or get killed. Pick your poison."

"Don't say that," Jasmine frowned.

"It's true."

Jasmine walked over to the couch and put her purse down. "Well, he wants me to move in with him."

"What? Already? That was quick, don't you think?"

"Yea it is, but we really have a crazy chemistry. It's working."

"You sure you want to put yourself in so deep in with a dope boy, though? I mean the shopping is all good, but you might really want to consider what comes with being with him. You're a loyal girl too. I know you. Your loyalty might be the death of you."

"Why would you say that? I'm not dying," Jasmine snapped back.

"I don't mean literally, although it could be taken that way too. I'm just saying you're going to be put in situations where you have to ride for him and it might be at the cost of your innocence or wellbeing."

"You're always so negative when I talk about him and you haven't even met him," Jasmine frowned.

"I'm just looking out and besides, you really gonna bounce on me and leave me to pay this rent on my own? I didn't get a job after graduation, you did," Jess complained.

"Well, I mean he said he would pay my half of the rent for up to six months until you could find someone to replace me," Jasmine encouraged her to agree.

"This guy must really make money. I thought he was just some small time guy, but to pay your rent where you're not even living is boss." Jess was impressed.

"Girl, he said he made 1.5 million last year," Jasmine gushed.

"Oh yeah, he selling more than some weed. Damn! Well if he's going to pay the rent then I really can't stop you. I just want you to be careful, of course."

"Don't worry about me, I'm good," Jasmine reassured. "He's very protective of me anyway. I feel safe with him."

Jess sighed as she knew that same life. It was nothing new to her and she knew exactly what Jasmine was about to walk into. Ride or die wasn't a term for no reason. It was real. The women in relationships with these guys always suffer in one way or another. They are usually the forgotten ones. Nobody cares about them or pays them any mind. They are often used by the man to commit crimes because they are women and less of a suspected target. Most times, it works too, but sometimes it doesn't. Jess hated the idea of having Jasmine in that risky situation, but she warned her, especially with how naïve and inexperienced she was. Jasmine was never exposed to this type of stuff growing up, so it worried her even more. She seemed to be more and more excited about the lifestyle the more she was exposed to it. It was the life she saw on movies and TV shows, but instead, it was really happening to her. If she knew better, she would be distancing herself from it. She was going to have to learn on her own because she didn't seem to be listening to the advice given to her. Jess wasn't about to make a grown ass woman do something she didn't want to do. She spoke her opinion twice and that's all she was going to say about it.

Jasmine loaded all her bags into her bedroom and started to unpack her stuff. She hung up the clothes and stacked her shoe boxes in her closet. Once she finished unpacking and hanging her new stuff up, she laid down on her bed, exhausted from her day. She smiled to herself as she thought about Fox. She imagined living in that big house of his and driving a nice car like his. She wanted the luxurious lifestyle, but knew nothing of the hard work that came with it. She knew nothing of the violence and stress it came with. The risk and lack of trust that came with it.

The two girls made martinis in the kitchen and plopped down on the sofa. They started talking about everything from work, school, friends and of course, the topic of men. Jasmine couldn't stop gushing over Fox and while Jess didn't like it, she liked to see her friend happy, so she entertained the conversation.

"But you said he made 1.5 mil, though?" Jess said grinning.

"Yea," Jasmine laughed at her friend. "See now you see what I see."

"I mean that's a lot of money."

"Yea, I had no idea. His house and car are nice, but not 1.5 million nice."

"Well, you know, he might be smart. He can't be flashy and spending it all crazy. That's how the Feds start watching you. He's probably trying to stay low-key."

"Yea, he saves a lot. I been to one of his stash spots."

"Word? He let you know where the stash spot was? He must really like you."

"I found out on accident. Don't get too excited," Jasmine complained.

"How you find out on accident?"

"I followed him." Jasmine laughed.

"What? You stalking this man now?"

"No! I left my charger at his house and we left out at the same time. My phone was dead so I couldn't call him and I saw him at the light and just followed him a few blocks down by the corner store, near that parking lot on Arch Street. He was going in there and I saw him meet his boy there. His boy had his gun out, so I was freaking out. He told me he had it out because that was a private spot for them."

"Damn, so he didn't want you to know?"

"Nope."

"Oh well, you know now!" Jess said and stuck her tongue out.

The rest of the night flew by and the two girls were three martinis in each. They laughed and joked as they slowly got up and went into their own bedrooms and got ready to sleep. When Jasmine got into bed, she called Fox to check on him. He was out with Joey and Chuck, handling business, so she told him to have a safe night and hung up. She put her phone down and in three seconds, picked it right back up. She called Fox back.

"Babe. I want to sleep with you tonight," she whined into the phone.

"I just dropped you off," he laughed.

"I know, but I can't sleep here. I just wanna be in your bed."

"I'm not even home, though. I just told you I'm out with Joey and Chuck."

"When will you be done?"

"I'm not sure. You wanna just come by and sleep there anyway?" he suggested.

"I just want you to put me to sleep." She grinned so hard he could see it through the phone.

"Oh really?" His dick jumped.

"Yea, babe. Just come let me in the house and fuck me real good, then you can go back out and handle whatever you want. When you come back home, I'll be sleep in the bed."

"Aight, I'll head back to the crib now. Meet me there."
Fox hung up the phone.

Jasmine got up and showered quickly, rubbed her body
down with cocoa butter, finished it up with perfume, and then
threw on some sweats. She left her room, put on her sneakers
and grabbed her purse, when Jess came out of her room, half
asleep.

"Where your hoe ass going?" Jess said.

"Girl bye. I'm going to Fox's place." Jasmine laughed
and waved her friend off.

"Ok thot. You know it's 1 a.m.?"

"Yes! I know it's booty call hours. I'm going to get
some dick. Anything else?"

They laughed together and Jasmine left. Jess stretched
and sat on the couch with her cell phone. She scrolled through
her contacts in her phone and tapped one. As it rang, she picked
at her nails nervously.

"Yo'," the voice on the other end said.

"My bad I had to hang up earlier, but I got a job for
you," she declared.

"Word? Talk to me," Jay replied.

"You know the deal; I need my cut."

"Of course. You like family, I always look out. You did
a favor for my brother; I could never forget what you did for
us."

"It wasn't even a favor. I did what needed to be done at
that moment."

"That too. So what's up?"

"I got some good info on where some niggas been
stashing their money. It should be an easy come up as long as
they not there at the time."

"Cool. Cool. Send me the location. We will watch it. See the routine."

"Well, I don't know the exact address, but I know it's on top or behind that corner store on Arch. The one near that big empty ass parking lot that's been closed off."

"Oh yeah, I know that store. Shit, I wonder if there's another way up in there besides the store entrance."

"Yeah, it gotta be. Let me know when it go down so I know you safe."

"I got you. How you been holding up?" he asked concerned.

"I've been ok. I just been missing Bop, ya know? Every time I go visit him in there, I get angry again. I could shoot that nigga over and over and over again." Jess felt her heart sinking in her chest at the thought.

"I feel you. The lawyer ain't even been telling us shit. He just beat around the bush. Fuck we paying you for then?" Jay yelled.

"Right. Anytime I call him, he says he will get back to me."

"That nigga fucked Bop over real bad. Snitch ass nigga."

"I heard he still in a coma."

"I hope he never wakes up. I heard its real bad."

"Good. I shoulda shot him one more time."

"Savage," he laughed.

"You know I would do anything for Bop. That is my heart."

"I know. You family now, don't you ever forget that."

"What if he wakes up?" Jess' tone of voice changed.

67

"Don't worry about that. He won't, and if he does, I'll take care of it," he assured her before hanging up. "He doesn't have any idea who you are anyway."

When Jasmine arrived at Fox's house, he was just pulling up as well. Perfect timing for them both. They walked into the house and before he could even close the door, Jasmine was reaching down to unbuckle his belt and button on his jeans. He returned by grabbing her by the waist, pulling her up against his body. She smelled fresh and he couldn't wait to shove his tongue in between her legs.

They kissed and exchanged not only their tongues, but every emotion in their bodies through the passion in that kiss. He picked her up as he reached behind her and locked the front door. He effortlessly carried her upstairs to the bedroom and laid her on the bed. She pulled her sweat pants off and revealed her pink lace panties. He wrapped his arms under her ass, pulled her body close to him and kneeled down on the bedroom floor, near the end of the bed. His lips touched every part of her thighs, up to her stomach and around her pussy that was begging for him to touch it. She squirmed with every touch of his lips to her body and moaned slightly. The anticipation was killing her and she started taking off her panties and he grabbed them and ripped them off.

"Damn babe, I liked that thong," she joked with a pout.

He stuck his tongue in her and her laugh turned into a moan. He pulled it out and began to circle around her clit until she was squirming away from him. She was sensitive and the pleasure was becoming too much, so he switched direction and flicked his tongue up and down. The sheets were nearly off the bed because of the grip she had on them, and she rocked her hips up and down on his face. A continued rhythm got her

68

closer and closer, until she grabbed his head and rubbed herself into his face, until she reached an orgasm. She laid there panting, trying to catch her breath and steady her heartbeat, while he took off his jeans and boxers.

His dick stood tall and full, so he climbed on top of her and shoved it into her mouth. In and out of her he pumped it, as she fought hard not to gag on the size of it. He lifted her head with his hand and guided himself deeper. So deep, she couldn't help but gag, and with each gag came more saliva. He face fucked her until she had tears coming out of her eyes and he looked down at her beautiful face swallowing his dick. The image made him tense up and release all the way down her throat. He slid out of her mouth and she swallowed it and wiped her mouth clean. In a rush, he pulled up his boxers and put his jeans back on, while she got under his blanket and rolled over.

"Babe, I gotta run back out. I'll be back soon and when I do, I'm going to slide up in that pussy." Fox grabbed his keys and cell phone and headed out. She was half asleep before he even made it to the front door.

Fox hopped in his car when his phone rang. He looked at it and saw it was Joey and threw it into his passenger side seat. He was on the way and didn't need him rushing him about it. He pulled down his mirror and checked his face for his girl's residue around his mouth. All clear. He started the car and drove out to meet with his boys. As soon as he walked up, Chuck was leaning on his car and looked up. He began to walk to him and Joey opened the passenger side door and hopped out.

"I called your phone like five times. Where the fuck you been at?" Joey yelled as he walked towards him.

"I told y'all I had something to handle and would be right back," Fox dismissed him.

"Rev awake," Chuck said calmly.

"Word?" Fox got excited. This was good news that he needed to hear. "He aight?"

"We don't know, man. It's the middle of the night; they ain't letting nobody in that bitch right now," Joey said.

"Right, right. You know what time visiting hours is? We gotta be the first ones there," Fox said.

"I think they start 8 a.m. I hope his mom not still tripping," Chuck said.

"Fuck her. I'm going to see my boy. First thing in the morning, we there," Fox said and the three of them walked into the store and up the stairs.

*   *

"Why we gotta come here so early, though?" he complained.

"Because we need to know the schedule. When they go in and when they go out. Common sense, nigga." Bop's brother, Jay, explained to his young boy, Kyle.

Kyle sucked his teeth, got comfortable in his seat, closed his eyes and relaxed. He knew it was going to be a long day of sitting and waiting. Wasn't his idea of a come up if he had to wait around all day for it. He would rather run up in there, wave his gun around and leave with bags of money, but Jay knew better. Jay was smarter and always prepared, especially after his brother got locked up. He was taking no chances of making even the smallest mistake and getting caught up. He feared nothing but he didn't want the same fate as Bop and did everything he could to avoid it…except be legal. The two brothers were born into the streets by a father who was still in it. The cycle was continuous and normal for them all; there was no other option.

Kyle opened his eyes and took a look at the store, then shook his head and closed them again. He didn't even know what they were supposed to be looking for. There was nigga after nigga going in and out of the store. They all looked the same, all dressed the same and all probably did the same shit they did. There was no way to tell whose spot they were even staking out.

"So you not even going to help? You just gonna lay there, sleep? Fuck you come for then?" Jay said with an attitude.

"What you want me to do?" Kyle asked confused.

"Look at each and every single person that goes in and out. See who spends a long time in there. See who returns more than once. Come on, man. How you supposed to be a man of the streets and you can't even use simple common sense to rob someone."

Jay was getting annoyed and realized he made a mistake bringing Kyle. He had to split the money with someone who wasn't even any help. He was only help when it came to waving a gun in someone's face. He was perfect at that shit, but it takes more than being a tough guy; you gotta be smart too.

*   *

At 7:45 a.m., Fox, Chuck and Joey walked up to the hospital entrance a little nervous, but excited to see Rev. They all knew his mom was probably there again, but they were

71

going to make sure they got through to him this time, no matter what. They had to know what happened and if he was ok. Fox was determined and wouldn't leave until he saw him. Inside the waiting room, they waited patiently until 8 a.m., with no sign of his mother or anyone else waiting for him. She could be in his room already, though, who knows. Fox got up a few minutes before 8 and walked over to the front desk to ask about Rev.

"Hey, how you doing? I want to visit Revanald Howard," Fox said to the petite little woman who sat behind the desk in her hospital smock.

"Visiting hours start at 8," she replied without even looking up.

"Ok, it's 7:58. Can we sign in now?" Fox asked.

"Sure. The sign in sheet is right there in front of you. Let me look up his room for you." She began to type the name into the computer and then paused.

"Oh, I'm sorry. He is a high-security patient and is only allowed approved visitors."

"Shit," Fox said under his breath.

She looked up from the computer for the first time at Fox after hearing him curse. "I'm sorry, it's hospital policy, and for his safety."

"That's my best friend, though," Fox pleaded.

"Well, what is your name, maybe you're on the list?" She clicked on his name on the computer. "Yea, I'm sorry, he only has one name on the list and it looks like his mother or someone related."

"Is there any way you can go ask him if he can add me and my boys to the list. I know he would want to see us. He just woke up from a coma."

"Sir, I can't do that. He has to provide his list."

"Please. I need to see him. He's been in a coma for over a week now. What can we do?"

"I'm sorry I can't do anything," she frowned. "I really am sorry."

"Yeah, me too." Fox turned to walk away disappointed, then stopped. "What if you just asked him. No one would have to know. I won't tell anyone and you can keep it to yourself as well. And when we leave, you make an extra five hundred dollars."

She lifted her head and looked at Fox through the top of her glasses. She was now intrigued and interested. Five hundred dollars never hurt anybody, she thought. She stared at him for a moment, trying to think if this was a good idea. If something happened to this man, then it would be her fault, but all she had to do was add their names to the approved list if he did actually approve them. She weighed the pros and cons in her head as quickly as possible and came to her conclusion.

"Write your names on this paper. I'll take it back to him and check on his approval. He has to approve all of y'all first," she said firmly and slid over a pen and a piece of scrap paper.

He wrote down all three of their names and slid the paper back over to her. She picked it up and told someone near the door to watch the desk. She headed back to his room and walked in. There was a nurse inside cleaning up from his breakfast. The petite woman approached his bed and looked him over. He looked weak, but in his right mind.

"Hey, I have a couple visitors for you, but they're not on your visitor list. I'm not supposed to be doing this, but they insisted they were your best friends. I need your approval before I allow them back." She handed him the paper with the three names on it.

He looked them over and a small smile formed on his sunken in face. "Of course. Let them through."

"Ok. I'll be sending them back." She smiled and thought about the five hundred dollars she was about to make.

When she returned, the three of them were waiting at the desk for her. She smiled a huge smile and asked them to all show ID and sign in on the sheet. Fox pulled out the money and handed it to her as he walked by. She smiled and sat back down and watched them walk back.

"My niggggga!" Fox said as he walked into the room and saw his ace laid up. "You in here living and shit." They laughed.

"What took y'all so long?" Rev complained.

"Nigga, you was sleep!" Joey reminded him.

"How you feeling? You aight, man? We were all worried," Chuck added.

Rev slowly sat up to see his visitors better. He was still in pain and it showed. He moved slow and calculated to avoid any pressure points of pain. "I'm good. I'm just happy to be alive. I thought I was dead."

"Damn. What the doctors say? You gonna be ok? When you getting outta here?" Joey asked.

"He said they are still running test, but everything has been coming out good so far. I can be out of here in a week if everything heals up right," Rev answered.

"So what happened, man? Who did this to you?" Fox cut to the chase. Now that they knew his health status, it was time to get to the revenge part. You don't shoot someone and just walk away unscratched. It wasn't happening, Fox thought to himself.

"I don't even know. All I remember is coming from work and I was at the gas station, paying, and then I went back out to my car. I was about to pump the gas and someone came up on me. It was dark and I didn't recognize her. It was a girl."

"A girl? Are you fucking serious?" Chuck yelled.

They all looked at Rev like he had two heads. It's not every day that women were out in their neighborhood bussing guns. On top of that, why would a woman shoot him? He was actually the only one in the group who had a girlfriend and was faithful. They just had a son four months ago and everything seemed to be good with them, so it wasn't any relationship drama.

"Damn, what did you do to the jawn?" Joey joked.

"I didn't do anything to nobody. I just walked out to my car and she started bussing. She didn't say shit and she didn't do nothing else. Bitch shot me two times," Rev complained.

"This don't even make sense," Fox added. "There's gotta be more to it."

"Would you recognize her on the street?" Chuck asked.

"Oh yea, I definitely would."

*   *

"Wait, wait. I seen them already go in today," Kyle sat up in his seat to get a better look out the car window.

"Which ones? Those three right there?" Jay asked.

"Yea! They went in before."

"Oh shit. That's them niggas Fox and them." Jay recognized them right away.

"Who is that?" Kyle asked.

75

"Damn, you don't know shit, do you? They be moving heavy weight and that's Rev's people too."

"Oh shit? That's Rev people?"

"Yea! Small ass world," Jay said. "I wonder how Jess knew their stash spot."

"Don't matter. What matter is we about to make a come up," Kyle said and prematurely grabbed his gun.

"You are right about that. I know they got some good cash up in there."

Kyle shook his head in agreement and opened his passenger car door. Before he could even get it halfway open, Jay grabbed him by the arm and pulled him back in.

"What are you doing? They still in there stupid!" Jay yelled at Kyle.

"So we go in there, tell them we taking the money and be out," Kyle argued.

"No. Listen, everything don't gotta be a scene out a movie. Chill out. We can just wait till they leave and go in there," Jay reasoned.

Kyle sucked his teeth, "Fine."

After sitting in the car for another forty-five minutes, waiting, they saw the three men exit the store. Jay watched intensely as they walked to two separate cars and got in and pulled off. Jay and Kyle pulled on their black gloves and placed their hoods over their heads, then hopped out the car with guns in hand. They crept to the back of the building for an alternative door and found one that was locked. There was a glass window on the door and Jay took a rock and bashed the glass in. He reached in carefully and jiggled the lock open. Easy access, he thought.

Jay pulled the door open and peeked inside, making sure no one was there. It was empty and dark, but the light on the back of the building illuminated the immediate hallway up to the steps. Once they started going up the steps, it got darker, and Kyle pulled out the flashlight on his iPhone. They went up the flight of steps more quickly and encountered another door that was locked. Kyle was an expert locksmith and could pick just about any lock. He pulled out a credit card from his jean pocket and began to slide it up and down near the knob until he was able to unlock it. Just a trick he learned on the streets.

Inside, they walked slowly, letting their eyes adjust to the dark. Once acclimated to the environment and lighting they began to look for where the money would be. In ten minutes of searching, they got frustrated. It was dark, but they didn't want to turn the light on for fear that someone would notice it. Jay stood still and looked around the room, trying to figure out where it would be. He walked around the outline of the room and felt the walls. All seemed to be solid, so he started looking up at the ceiling. Nothing looked out of the ordinary, so he began to look at the floor. There was a throw rug in front of a tan sofa that he noticed and went for it. He pulled it out the way and there was a cut out on the wooden panels on the floor.

"I got it," Jay said and Kyle walked over.

The two of them pulled up the wooden panels one by one to reveal stacks of black bags, duffle bags. Jackpot. Kyle reached in and unzipped one and inside were rubber bands full of money. The bags were full to capacity and there were about ten bags. Kyle zipped the bag up and pulled it out and continued grabbing more. Jay followed behind him, pulling one bag out after another. They grabbed as many bags as they could carry and ran out, down the steps and back outside. It took them two trips, but they cleaned them out and made it out of there before anyone noticed.

Chapter 6

Don't Trust Her

On my way back to the house, I looked at my cell phone. I had a 911 text from both Chuck and Joey, so I immediately had a bad feeling. We only text 911 if it's really important. I called Chuck right back to find out what was wrong.

"Yo', nigga. Meet me at the A spot, now," he said as soon as he answered.

"Everything ok?" I asked.

"No, and that's all I'm going to say."

I hit a U-turn and headed towards our A meet up spot. We had about five spots that we worked out of. We kept it between me, Chuck, Joey, Greg and Rev. We called them the A, B, C, D, and E spots so only we knew which one was where. When I pulled up, I saw Chuck's car, but not Joey's car. I had a habit of scouting out my surroundings wherever I went. I always needed to know who was around and what I was walking into. The A spot was our first spot we claimed when we first started hustling. We kept a little cash there and sometimes met up just to package and handle business. There was not much use for it as it was a smaller area and we upgraded to different places since then. However, it was a good meeting place because it was the closest to all of us. I walked inside and saw both Chuck and Joey, so I assumed they drove in together.

"What's good?" I asked as I approached them and showed them love.

"The money is gone," Joey blurted out.

"What? What money?" I was confused.

"Nigga, the money we stashed here," Chuck replied.

I ran over to check where we kept our money under the floor boards and it was gone. Empty. I stood there for a minute, thinking. All kinds of thoughts ran through my head. I had to get them together before I could even say a word. I was shocked and pissed and the anger was taking over. My blood was boiling. I was ready to fuck someone up.

"Tell me all our money not gone?" I stabilized myself long enough to ask.

"Just this spot. Someone knows our shit. We just went and grabbed up the rest and put it in my crib before they got to those too. We didn't take the school stash, though. We checked and it was still good, but we left that there."

"Who the fuck knows our locations?" I paced back and forth, thinking. "Come on, we gotta go to your crib in case they try to get the rest."

We rushed out and headed to Chuck's crib with guns loaded and prepared. I tried to mentally calculate how much money they had to have taken and I was thinking it was about seventy-five thousand dollars. I was hoping I was wrong and it was less. I was hoping that I miscalculated the amounts in each stash spot. I was hoping I was dead ass wrong.

"How much?" I asked as we hopped out the cars and headed into his house. Nobody answered.

"No one knows? Or y'all just can't fucking hear?" I asked with an attitude.

"Rev was the last to count it, but I think it was about eighty thousand the last time I did."

"Shit." I sucked my teeth. "Hold the fuck up. Who noticed the shit was gone?"

"Joey did and called me, then we went to spot B to check there and then all the ones after that," Chuck answered.

I grabbed Joey up by the neck and slammed him against the front of Chuck's house and pushed my gun to his head. "What was you doing at the spot? We didn't have any schedule drops or meetings."

"Yo', Fox, chill out. That's Joey. You know he ain't take that shit."

"I went by there to check on shit. Fuck you mean? Get this gun out my face!" Joey tried to wiggle out of my grip. I loosened up, then pushed back.

"Man, my bad. I'm fucked up right now," I apologized.

"We boys. We brothers. You putting a gun to my head? What type of shit is that?" Joey was pissed.

"I said my bad. This shit don't make no fucking sense. How are people going missing and our money? What is going on? Rev got shot and we don't have any idea who did it. Some bitch!" I was dead ass confused and looking for answers.

"I don't know. I'm just as lost as you." Chuck opened the front door and led us to the rest of our money in his basement.

"I knew something was going on, so I checked on the money. That's all. With Rev and Greg shit up in the air, I just knew something was wrong," Joey said. "Nothing's being done!"

"Fuck you want us to do?" I questioned, as I pulled the bags of money out and took a seat. "Let's count this shit up. I need to know what we got left exactly."

"Look, this shit ain't no joke. I'm not just trying to wait around for one of us to turn up missing or shot either," Joey replied.

"I hear you," I replied. Everyone always turned to me for the answers but this time, I didn't have any. Joey was right and something had to be done. We couldn't just wait around for the next hit to happen, whether it was us or our money.

"So what y'all want to do?" I asked.

"Show them niggas we ready for war. They bitching us right now," Joey said.

"We gotta be sure it's them," I reminded him.

"Fuck that, let's just move on them. It gotta be them." Joey was hyped up.

"We don't know that," I pleaded.

"Well, who the fuck else is it?" Joey argued. "Nothing else even makes sense."

"You right," I gave in.

*   *

Jasmine rolled over and stretched out on the bed. She pulled the blanket up to cover her exposed breasts and closed her eyes. The soft sheets and comfy blanket made her instantly relax. She reached over and grabbed her cell phone and pushed the home button to see what time it was. In and out of sleep, she waited for Fox to return to the house.

Eventually, she fell into a deep sleep, forgetting about her man coming back. The next time she woke, it was a stream of daylight coming in from behind the curtain. Once she noticed Fox was still not in the bed, she sat up quickly, looking around the bedroom. It didn't look like he ever came back. She grabbed her phone and texted him 'WYA?', and waited for a reply. She got up and brushed her teeth and slid back in bed and checked her phone every thirty seconds. Her nerves were bad because of the lifestyle he lived. The thought that something was wrong was constantly running through her head.

After waiting five minutes with no reply, she called his phone and got no answer. Now fully worried, she sat up and called again. Still no answer. She looked out the window and saw his car pulling up. A wave of relief overcame her as she threw her phone on the bed and got back under the covers. When he walked into the room, he was silent as she watched him as he sat on the edge of the bed. He sat there and said nothing.

"Baby, you ok?" she asked and sat up slightly, up against the pillow.

"Did you tell anyone about where you followed me to the other day?" he asked without even looking at her.

"Where?" she asked confused, and sat up and moved over next to him.

"Where I hide my money. Where you met me to tell me you left your charger."

"No, I didn't say anything about that." She shook her head no.

Fox jumped up, grabbed her by the neck and threw her up against the wall. Her head banged on the wall and she fell to the ground. He rushed over and picked her up by her hair and pressed her against the wall.

"Don't fucking lie to me." Fox got closer to her face. "Tell the truth!"

83

"Fox, I don't know what you're talking about. I didn't tell anyone!" she cried.

"You playing games." He shoved her down to the ground.

"I told you I don't know what you're talking about."

"You're lying. Who did you tell?" he screamed down at her.

She shielded her face in anticipation of being hit. "No one!"

He kicked her and walked away. "I know you're lying."

He picked up her clothes that laid at the foot of the bed on the floor. After throwing them at her, he picked up her shoes and threw them too. She cried on the floor, unable to even put together what just happened. Her mind was racing and she was in shock that he put his hands on her. He was so angry and she never saw him this way. He walked out the room and slammed the door shut behind him.

She quickly began to get dressed and picked up the remainder of her belongings. She was sure not to forget her charger, purse and phone, and headed to the door. Still shaken up, she wasn't sure if she should try to talk to him more or just leave, but she had no choice as he was coming back up the stairs when she was at the top.

He walked up and grabbed her and pulled her close to his chest. "I didn't mean to hit you."

"Didn't mean to? Well you did!" Jasmine caught an attitude while tears continued to stream down her face.

"Look, I am sorry. I shouldn't have hit you, but I need to know who you told about my spot," he said and stepped back.

"I told you, no one." She pushed passed him and started down the steps.

"You're the only person who knew," he explained. "No one else knew but you, and a day later, my shit goes missing?"

"How many times I gotta say I don't know?" She caught an attitude as she looked back up at him.

"I think you're lying. Get the fuck out of here," he spat back at her and waved her off.

She continued down the steps and out the front door. He followed behind her angrily and closed the door behind her. He was pissed and wanted to really beat her ass. He felt bad for hitting her, but wanted to hit her even more. He knew she said something; it was too much of a coincidence that this happened. He worked too hard for his money and to have someone take it from him was eating him up.

She got into her car and cried harder and harder now that she was alone. She couldn't believe that he hurt her and accused her. The pain she felt was numbing as she drove home, barely paying attention to the road. Once she got there, she parallel parked into her spot and sat in her car, crying it out.

Once she finally got the energy to get out the car and go inside, she still had tears rolling down her face. Inside, she went straight to her bedroom and slammed the door shut and continued to cry in private. Her bed felt soft and it welcomed her when she felt like she had no one. She was so hurt and didn't know what to think. Her mind raced as she thought about her and Fox being over. She couldn't forgive him for hitting her and he was so mad at her she didn't think he would even want to. She laid there in the dark, staring at the ceiling so long the tears on her face dried and she eventually fell asleep.

When she woke up, she heard Jess in the kitchen, cooking breakfast. She could smell the turkey bacon and rolled over and stretched. Realizing she never ate dinner last night, her stomach growled as she forced herself out the bed. She walked into the kitchen half asleep, but ready for some food, but Jess turned around and stopped in her tracks.

"What happened to your face?" Jess put the pan down on the counter, off the heat, and rushed over to her.

Completely forgetting she got hit in the face, she reached up and touched it and flinched at how sore it was. She was suddenly fully awake and aware. She headed to the bathroom to check the mirror. As she stared at herself and the purple-blue bruise on her face that surrounded her once beautiful, angelic eyes, she began to cry. Jess stood behind her, asking what happened repeatedly, but she couldn't get the words out to even speak. She looked back up at her face and leaned in closer to the mirror to get a better look. The pain she felt in her heart was way more than the bruise on her face. Her ego was bruised. Her womanhood was taken from her. She was embarrassed and felt so small. How could Fox do this to her, she wondered.

"Are you going to tell me what happened? Who hit you?" Jess continued to question her.

Jasmine walked out the bathroom angry. "I don't want to talk about it."

"You have a huge bruise on your face. You need to tell me what happened," Jess insisted.

"I really don't want to talk about it. I'm ok," Jasmine replied and grabbed a cup out of the cabinet and got the orange juice out of the refrigerator.

86

"Ok, fine. I only thought I was your best friend," Jess said with an attitude.

"You know what Jess, I don't need this right now." She slammed her cup down and went back to her bedroom and shut the door.

"Whatever," Jess said under her breath and finished her food.

After her food was done, she anxiously got dressed and headed out. She rushed and made her way over to Jay's house. When she parked, she hopped out and banged on the door. Jay looked through the window first before opening the door for her. Her eyes darted around the room for the money as soon as she walked in.

"Where is it at?" Jess asked.

"Damn, hi Jess. How are you? I'm doing good," Jay joked as he closed the door behind her and locked it.

"My bad," she laughed and took a seat on his couch that sunk way down. "You need a new couch with all this money you just got. This shit is broken."

"It ain't broken, it's worn with love," Jay joked again. He was in a good mood, clearly.

Kyle walked out the kitchen with a bottle of Sprite in his hand and a blunt in his other. He nodded his head to Jess and exhaled some smoke. Jay ran up the stairs and returned with a book bag that he put next to Jess' feet. She smiled and quickly unzipped it. She ran her hands through the money, trying to count it with her eyes.

"How much is this?" she questioned.

"That's fifteen thousand."

"Damn nigga! Yaaaaaas! That is a come up. So y'all must have done good then, huh?" Jess exclaimed.

"Yeah, it was good. I made sure I gave you a nice amount, though. I can't ever let you want for anything. You forever family. We hold each other down. Plus, you put me on to the spot."

"No doubt. I will always come to you with the info."

"I talked to Bop this morning. I'm going to go see him this weekend, if you want to go with me," Jay informed her.

"Yea. Of course. How is he doing?"

"He is always worried about you. I told him I got you, but he is worried about that nigga recently waking up. He thinks he might snitch or come after you."

"He has no clue who I am, where I am, or why he even got shot to begin with."

"Nah, a nigga knows. You out there snitching on niggas you gonna get murked. It's law. He knows exactly why he got hit. He knows he's a snitch, he just don't know you, and that's why it worked out."

"What happens when the cops start asking questions over here?"

"Nothing. I don't have nothing to do with it. They not going to think you!"

Jess zipped her book bag back up, stood up and threw it over her shoulder. "Ok, I trust you."

She started to walk to the door and stopped. She realized they may have a problem with the whole situation. She was playing it really close to home and being risky, but Jess was all about risk; she lived on the edge. Nothing like Jasmine.

"Oh yea, my girl came home all bruised up. I think her man knows she snitched, but she didn't say nothing to me about it." She turned to face Jay.

"What the fuck? Why you didn't tell me that's how you got the info. That's traceable back to you. You bugging. You better lay all the way low with that money then. If she starts seeing you spending a little more than usual, she's going to think back to who she mentioned it to."

"I know. I'll be careful. I'm her best friend; she's not going to think I told anyone. I can convince her that her nigga just got robbed by someone random. He a street nigga. It happens!"

"You right. Hit me if you need me and don't forget this weekend."

"I could never forget. I'll hit you up," Jess said as she opened the door and left the house with her newly found come up.

She didn't want to even go back home because Jasmine was probably still laying around, in her feelings, so she called a friend and made plans to go have lunch and have some drinks. She wanted to low-key celebrate with a couple drinks. She kept the book bag in her trunk and headed into the lounge.

When Fox finally got himself calmed down enough to think about what really happened, he still wasn't completely calm. He was angrier than anything and he wanted to kill whoever went in his spot. He cared about the money, but the disrespect alone was enough to make someone lose their life.

After Jasmine left, he paced back and forth, running different scenarios through his head. He didn't want to think Jasmine would set him up. She didn't seem like that type of girl and he didn't even think she knew the right kinds of people to pull it off. He dismissed the idea plenty of times in his head that it was her, but it kept running back to his mind that she knew the spot. It could have been any random nigga who may have been watching them. He didn't want to believe that he was that careless either. The denial was running deep and causing him more confusion than help. He needed to clear his mind, so he decided to go visit Rev at the hospital again. Talking to his friend that he almost lost was a sure way to ease his mind.

Once he got to the hospital, he was hoping Rev's mom was not there again. He walked in cautiously and looked around the lobby and did not see her. He walked up to the lobby sign in and saw the familiar face of the receptionist he tipped off before. His name should still be on the list, so he knew it wouldn't be a problem this time. She smiled brightly at him and said he could sign in and go right in. After walking past her and approaching his room, he stood outside of it. He wanted to calm himself down first before he upset Rev with any bad news. Greg was missing and Fox still never told Rev, and he definitely didn't want to upset him even more with this news of missing money. He just wanted to see his friend.

"Hey, man," Fox announced.

"Fox, what's up, man?" Rev smiled as he watched Fox walk in and take a seat next to his bed.

"Just came by to check on you. How you feeling?"

"I'm getting better. More energy today than yesterday."

"That's good to hear."

"I'm just bored as hell. I'm ready to get out of here."

"You'll be outta here soon. Don't worry about it. I'll come by every day until you are."

"Fox, you know I love you for that. Real talk. I respect you being here for me."

"You know I got you. Don't even worry about it."

"I know, man. I gotta ask you for a favor, though. I really didn't want to do this, but I have to." Rev looked away. His pride was hurting to ask for a favor.

"What's good?" Fox inquired.

"Listen, I been in here for a week after the shooting. I had surgery and was in that coma. I gotta stay here another five days to recover and rehabilitate before they release me."

"True. Gotta get right."

"You know I don't have no insurance, so these bills are high as hell and I have to pay them out of pocket. Ya know?"

"Damn, I didn't even think about insurance. You was supposed to sign up for that Obama care. You ain't do that shit?"

"I don't be paying attention to shit like that. I heard of it, but you know I don't have no legal job."

"That's the whole point. It is to help people with no job with insurance," Fox explained.

"Damn, I ain't know."

"Now you do," Fox laughed.

"Well, I was hoping that when I get out of here, you could front me some work so I could get back on my feet. I been out for a while and after paying all these bills, I'm going to be down. I got a baby to feed and my girl stressing me out every day, calling me about the bills that's coming to the house."

"Oh, damn. Say no more. I will put up the money for some extra work and give that to you. Then when you flip it, ya know, just get me back what you owe me; don't worry about anything extra. No interest," Fox offered. He didn't show how pissed he was at the request because he didn't want Rev to know he was also low on money since they got robbed. He still had other money stashed, but this was going to be another dent in it. There was no way Fox would let Rev be down and out, ever.

"Thank you, man. I knew I could count on you. Could you have it as soon as I get out? I'm trying to go right to work. Feel me?"

"Yeah, I'll make the call today to have it in five days, when you get out."

"Good looking," Rev said and leaned back comfortably on his pillow. He looked like a load of stress was just taken off of him.

"Well, I'm going to get out of here. I just wanted to stop in and check on you. I'll be back by tomorrow."

"Aight, thanks again. See you tomorrow."

Chapter 7

Your Crime is My Crime

    Jess finally decided to go back home and hoped Jasmine wasn't still being bitchy. When she first walked in, it was silent in the house, the lights were out and she assumed she was sleep. Her car was parked out front so she knew she was home. She walked quietly into the living room, through the family room, and to her bedroom and opened the door. She heard noise from Jasmine's room and she assumed she woke her up. She put her purse down and started taking her shoes off and undressing, when Jasmine appeared in the bedroom door. She threw her book bag into her closet nonchalantly.

    "Hey. I didn't mean to snap at you earlier," Jasmine apologized.

    "It's cool. I understand you were upset and emotional."

    "Yeah, I was. A lot of shit was running through my head. I've had time to calm down though and think rationally."

    "Good. Now you want to tell me what happened?"

    "First, I got a question that needs an honest answer."

    "Sure. What is it?" Jess asked.

    "Did you tell anyone about what I said about my dude having a secret spot, or did you go by there?"

    Jess looked at her confused. She played dumb and acted as if she was completely oblivious to what was going on. She deserved an Oscar for this scene she was about to put on. Award to the fakest bitch in a friendship scene goes to...

93

"What? Of course not. Why would I even do that? Is that what happened? He hit you?" Jess turned her face in disgust.

"He thinks I ran my mouth about it," Jasmine confessed.

"That piece of shit put his hands on you?" Jess threw her clothes down on the chair next to her bed.

"Someone robbed him."

"I don't give a fuck what happened. He shouldn't be hitting on you!"

"I know. It's crazy. I never saw that side of him."

"You shouldn't ever!" Jess walked closer to hug Jasmine. "You want me to go beat him up?" she smiled as she pulled away.

"He already apologized." Jasmine stood up for him.

"So? Fuck him."

"It's just weird. No one knew about his spot except his team and me and you."

"Well, maybe he got a rat on his team. Or, it could be anyone that knows they get money. They could have followed them."

"Yea, true." Jasmine looked down.

"Girl, pick your head up. This is not your fault. I told you that getting in too deep with this type of lifestyle has consequences."

"I know, but I don't need to hear I told you so right now. Damn, Jess."

"You're right. I'm sorry. My bad." Jess pulled out an oversized t-shirt from her dresser and pulled it over her head.

Jasmine stood there for a moment as Jess prepared for bed and walked over and hugged her. "Thanks, friend. Forgive me?"

"I love you, go to bed," Jess replied.

"I love you too," Jasmine said and went to her room and called it a night.

When Jasmine woke up, she decided to try to go talk with Fox. She had to clear the air and let him know that it wasn't her that snitched. She felt foolish trying to explain herself when she was the one who should be mad, but she couldn't help but try to clear her name. Once up and showered, she looked into the mirror at her bruise. It still looked terrible, so she grabbed some concealer and foundation and applied it as best she could. It looked a little better, but was still noticeable, so she grabbed a pair of sunglasses on the way out the door.

She pulled up to his house and rang the doorbell. Her nerves were driving her crazy as she anxiously waited for him to open the door. He looked surprised to see her as she stood there outside his front door. He didn't expect her to come by; he thought he would have to go to her if anything.

"Come in." He stepped to the side and allowed her to walk inside.

"Look, we need to talk," she said as she walked to his couch and sat down.

"We definitely do," Fox agreed and sat next to her.

"Look, I would never expose you to be robbed. That's not something I would ever do. I thought you trusted me and I thought you cared about me. You put your hands on me," Jasmine said and started to cry again.

"I know. I'm sorry, I just flipped. I thought it was you. I am so sorry. If I could take it back, I would." He stood up and went to the kitchen. When he came out, he had a vase with twenty-four beautiful, full red roses in it.

He handed them to her and she smiled, admiring them before putting the vase down on the coffee table. She stared at them and cried even more. She was still hurt that he hit her and didn't want to be in a relationship where this was ok. She didn't want him to think he could do it and just say sorry and everything would be ok, but she wanted him so badly. Her heart was with him.

"I'm sorry, Jazz. It will never happen again. I promise."

"Too many times I've heard sorry in a short amount of time, Fox." She continued to cry.

"I mean it, though. I never had a girlfriend before. This is new for me. I don't know how to handle my emotions sometimes."

"It's not fair to me."

"I know, baby. Please forgive me." He wrapped his arms around her as she continued to cry.

"I'm your girlfriend?" she whimpered out in between tears and snot.

"Yea. Baby, you my only girl." Fox tried his best to comfort her.

"Ok," she whined in approval.

He pulled her face up by the chin and kissed her. She slowly pulled back and took her sunglasses off and he saw the bruise poorly hidden under her makeup. His heart sank as he saw the realization of his actions last night. He wiped her tears away and kissed her on the lips again.

"I love you, baby. I'm sorry." He genuinely meant what he said.

"I love you too," she replied and hugged him even tighter.

They spent the next twenty minutes in each other's arms, holding each other in silence. They needed that healing time together and neither one of them wanted to move. The whole situation was crazy and they kept their friends out of it. It showed their loyalty to one another in her opinion. Fox never mentioned to his boys that he thought it could have been her who leaked the info and she appreciated it. Quickly getting over the pain she felt, she tried to enjoy the moment and him.

"Listen, my boy is coming home from the hospital in a week and I'm throwing him a little party. I know your birthday is coming up next week too. I want it to be for both of y'all and then after the party, take some time off work and I'll take you away for a few days. We can hit an island or something."

"Ok, that sounds good. Just let me know the exact dates of everything and I'll be there." Jasmine smiled.

"I want you to meet all my boys. Let them get familiar with you so you know, if anything ever goes down, they know you my other half."

"Ok, baby. Can I bring my roommate?"

"Of course. Bring whoever you want. It's your party too. But after our trip, I gotta tell you I'm going to be really busy. I have a lot going on right now and I have to focus on getting this money back up."

"I understand."

"Now on to other things. What's going on with you? How is the job?"

"It's great. My audiences have been loving my show. My manager has been giving me great compliments. I'm loving it."

97

"Good to hear. I know you out there killing it."

Later that day, Jasmine went home and began to pack all her stuff up. She decided to take Fox up on his offer to move in. Jess was pretty pissed that after he hit her, she still wanted to move forward with him, but there was nothing she could say to her to make her change her mind. She just let her know she was going to find out for herself what bad decisions she was making. By the time Jasmine had everything packed up, it was nightfall, and she had everything stuffed in her car and Fox's truck. They drove over and left everything in the cars until the morning; they were exhausted.

When the morning sun hit, Fox was up and ready to get his day started. He was motivated to make every day count and make that money back. His hunger returned with a vengeance after he accepted he would never see that money again. He wanted to make that 80k, plus a 20k profit, all before Rev returned home. He set goals and decided to work on them. He left early and Jasmine decided to begin unpacking her things. It took her all day, but she finally finished and got it all organized.

Fox met up with Joey and Chuck to go see Rev for the day. They met at the hospital and went in to see him. He was looking better every day they saw him. He looked healthier and happier and couldn't wait to get out of there.

"So where is Greg? He hasn't come by once to visit?" Rev asked. Silence came over the room as everyone looked at each other.

"We don't know," Fox finally said.

"Huh? What you mean?"

"Nobody knows where Greg went. He disappeared out of thin air. He's been gone for a little over a week now."

"What the fuck? No one's heard anything? When was the last time he was around?" Rev asked.

"No one knows shit. He went missing the night you got shot," Chuck chimed in.

"Damn. I gotta get outta here. Shit ain't right," Rev replied.

"Yea, when you come home, I'm throwing you a dope ass welcome home party, man. Fuck all this sad shit. You gotta celebrate beating that bullet," Fox tried to cheer him up and change the mood.

"Hell yea. I'm here for that!" he smiled.

"Also, it's my lady's birthday. I want y'all to meet her. I'm going to have her with me."

"Aw shit, look at you. Your lady?" Joey teased.

"Yeah, my lady, nigga," Fox shot back.

"Never thought I would hear you say that; Mr. Playa Pimp never has one girl. Wasn't you just fucking Kayla like yesterday?" Joey asked.

"Very funny. It wasn't yesterday," Fox defended himself.

"Ok, a week ago," Joey laughed and dapped Chuck up.

"Yeah, you moving quick with this one. You must really like her," Chuck added.

"I do, so respect her y'all, and look out for her too." Fox made it clear.

"Hey, if she right for you, I like her too," Chuck said.

"If she not right for you, I'm going to get that ass beat," Joey teased some more.

"That's not going down." Fox punched Joey in the arm.

"Ouch! Damn, I'm playing, man." Joey grabbed his arm in pain.

*   *

Jess was sitting at Jay's house, smoking a blunt with him, as they talked about Bop and memories of him; that was their mutual connection. Even though he was not dead, they kept his memory alive and present.

"I miss the shit out of him, man. I just wish he was still home with us," Jess said and pulled on the blunt and passed it to Jay.

"I know. Me too," Jay replied

"He will be home soon enough. At least we popped that rat ass nigga."

"Right. At least we got him. He should have died." Jay passed the blunt back after he took a pull. "But anyway, about them niggas we robbed; you know anywhere else they got money? Or anyone else? That job was love!"

"I know they got more money. He told my girl he made 1.5 million last year."

"Word?" Jay said and sat up. "Why you ain't tell me this before? We about to get that then."

"Yea. I don't know where else they hide it, though."

"We can follow them. It can't be that hard. We have to find out where they go and figure the shit out. It just might take some time and patience."

"I got all the time in the world for 1.5 mil." Jess laughed and pulled the last hit on the blunt, then put the tiny roach out in the ashtray on the table. "I want to go this time."

"Word? You want to be a big girl now?" Jay joked.

"I been a big girl since I pulled that trigger."

"Listen, I told Bop I would take care of you. This can be dangerous. You don't need it. I hit you with fifteen grand already. You just graduated college, ma; use that degree."

"Fuck that degree. I sent my resume out all over the state and not one interview. It's like I'm wasting my time. Everyone can't be like Jazz's smart, pretty ass. She got a job as soon as we graduated. I can make a quick come up doing this. I can take care of myself."

"You got what most of us can't get. Use that damn degree, Jess," Jay pleaded.

"Just let me get in on this. Me and you do the next job together," she insisted.

"Hell no. I need Kyle with me. I need that protection with me. I know you rough and tough, but I need another man with me too."

"Well fine, all three of us then."

"If you want to risk it then I'm down. I'm just letting you know, anything can happen."

"I know. I'm ready," Jess said confidently.

"Well ain't no better time than now," Jay said as he stood up and stretched his arms out. He began to put his sneakers on. "Kyle!" he yelled upstairs.

"What?" Kyle said as he came down the steps.

"Come on, we riding out. Got some plans," Jess said.

"Fuck we going?" Kyle replied.

"Store run first for these munchies," Jay laughed. "I'll explain the rest in the car."

Once the three of them left and got their snacks from the very storefront they robbed the money from the back of the other day, they sat in the car, eating. They figured that is where they

101

had to start to see the guys again and follow them. It was their only hope at the moment. Sit and wait.

*   *

Jasmine was back at Fox's house, cooking him dinner, when he walked in and sat on the couch on the phone. She was baking chicken and made rice with asparagus. It smelled good and the scent of the chicken had his stomach talking to him. He hung his phone call up and strolled into the kitchen and got a beer out of his refrigerator.

"It smells good."

"Thanks. I hope it tastes good." She checked the chicken in the oven, closed it and took a seat at the stool that sat at the kitchen island. Fox sat on the other side and put his beer down on the counter.

"I got an email today for my next story at work and it made me think of you. I have to do research on it and have my story ready on Monday."

"What's it about?" he inquired.

"The police have started trying to really crack down on drug trafficking locally. There is a big initiative to get a bunch of big dealers off the street. They're setting up raids and all types of stuff for a major sweep. They have already made some arrest."

Fox was caught off guard. He didn't expect that to be the topic and felt weird about her having to research that and report on it, but it was good to have an inside ear. He had no idea the cops were trying to crack down currently. He made a mental note to be careful on the streets and make sure he wasn't going to be caught up in that sweep.

102

"Damn. You going to do it?" he asked.

"Yea, I mean I don't have a choice. That is my assignment. I'm only telling you because I want you to be careful."

"Always." He smiled at her and drank some of his beer. "Listen, I think I should let you know some things about me."

"Yea? Like what?" Jasmine got scared.

"Nothing crazy. Don't make that face." He laughed. "In case anything ever happens to me, I want you to be cool. Ya know? Like if I ever get killed out here on these streets, I want you to have access to my money to take care of things with my boys and yourself."

"Oh God, Fox, don't talk like that."

"I mean even you said the cops are doing sweeps. I need to make sure if I get locked up, you can come bail me out, get me a lawyer and all that shit. You need to know where I keep the money."

"I mean I guess so. Now you trust me, huh?" She smiled.

"I guess I have to. You my girl. I gotta believe what you telling me."

"I would never do you dirty. You can trust me," she urged.

"Now if I tell you, you have to promise me you will not tell ANYONE and it's for emergencies only."

"Of course. I promise."

"Only if I need it. Not your emergencies, but my emergencies. Can I trust you with that responsibility?"

"Yes, babe. I got you. It's your money. I know."

"Aight," Fox said and looked her in the eyes. "This is going to sound crazy, but you know that closed down charter school near 5th Street, going towards the bridge?"

"Yea."

"I keep money in there."

"How the hell do you get in there?" Jasmine was confused.

"You have to climb up on the roof. It's not as hard as it sounds. It's the lower level part of the roof. There is a vent there that comes off easily. You go in that way, and it's in a blue locker, number 252."

"Oh lord, you going to have me climbing roofs?" Jasmine laughed.

"I know. It sounds crazy, but it's not too hard really. I just want you to know where it is. I'll keep the combination to myself. If you need it and you're able to ask me for it, then I'll give it to you, but if you can't get to me, then you can always cut off the lock."

"Ok. Hopefully, there will be no emergencies, babe. Then I won't have to turn into Spiderman and climb through a damn roof."

"Exactly. It's just a precaution. Is the food almost done? I'm starving!" He changed the subject.

"Yup. Should be done now."

As soon as he got his food, he devoured it like he'd never eaten before. He rushed through dinner and told her to get dressed. He wanted to go to his friend's house to play spades. His friend invited him over to hang out and have drinks and he wanted her to come. She got dressed quickly, wearing some cute but casual, and they headed out.

When they arrived at the house, it was more people there than they expected. "I thought you said a little get-together?" Jasmine asked.

"That is what he said. This a whole house party," Fox complained.

He wasn't in the mood to be around a whole lot of people, but he parked the car and they walked up to the house. When he walked in, the aroma of weed filled both of their noses and the heavy smoke and dim lights made it barely visible in there. The sound of his friend's booming, deep voice led the way to the kitchen, where he found him sitting at the table with cards, Henny bottles and people surrounding, watching the spades game.

"What up, Doc?" Fox said to his friend and leaned in and shook his hand and hugged him.

"Yo', Fox, you made it. I didn't think you would come. I never see you no more," Doc said as he returned the handshake.

"Yeah, you know I try to lay low when I can," Fox replied. He leaned in and gave Doc's girlfriend a hug and a kiss on the cheek. "Hey, Trina."

"Hey, Fox," she replied.

"This my girl, Jasmine," Fox introduced her to the room. Everyone smiled and waved or nodded their heads. She returned the smile.

"Hey, you want something to drink?" Trina asked Jasmine and led her to the other room for a cup and some of the punch she made earlier.

Fox found a corner of the kitchen counter and began to roll up his blunt, while Trina and Jasmine made drinks and chatted in the other room. He knew she was in good hands with her, so he took his time and started smoking. It was crowded in the kitchen, so he walked out and around to the family room to see who else was in the house. He didn't recognize many people because outside of his close friends, he tried to stay off the scene. Avoiding drama was the best possible way to stay off the radar and not get caught by police, robbed or shot. Those were his main goals of safety; to avoid those three things.

After walking around each room and greeting some familiar faces, he ended up back in the kitchen. Halfway through his blunt, he leaned up against the counter and relaxed. As soon as he did that, the front door of the house came busting open and a barrage of men in uniforms ran in, pointing guns. Instinct kicked in immediately and he ran and grabbed Jasmine's arm, yanking her so hard she dropped her cup of punch on the floor. He pushed through the small crowd of people to the back door and ran behind the shrubs behind his house. He stopped and ducked down and looked around for more cops. He didn't see any, so with her arm in his hand, he made a run for it to the next door neighbor's back yard and made their way to his car.

"Omg, what happened back there?" Jasmine said as she got into the car and Fox sped off quickly to blend in with traffic on the highway.

"Looked like a raid. Someone must have tipped them off that there was drugs there or something. I don't know."

"Crazy. It had to be a tip. I even saw a media truck parked, though."

"Forreal? That's wild. Like they knew they was going to come across something. That nigga doesn't even keep no work in his house; he not that stupid."

106

"This is crazy," Jasmine said, still shocked. "What are they going to do to him?"

"They just see a bunch of black people and automatically send the cops and the news."

"Right," Jasmine sucked her teeth. "I hope your friends are ok."

"They will be. He don't keep shit in his house. They gonna tear his place up looking for something they can't find and leave looking stupid."

While Jasmine and Fox settled in at home, Jess, Jay and Kyle still sat, surveillancing the stash spot. They finished their snacks hours ago and their high finally came down. Jess laid in the back seat, all the way down, while Kyle and Jay kept look out. Again, Jay was mad at the extra weight they had to carry and split the money between.

"This shit is wack. We gotta sit here all night?" Jess whined.

"Forreal. How long we gonna sit out here?" Kyle added.

"Unless y'all got a better idea on how to find these stash spots, we have to sit here and wait," Jay demanded.

"Look, let me just work it out of her. Maybe I can get her to slip up and mention it," Jess suggested.

"That shit ain't gonna work," Jay told her.

"I'm telling you. Just let me work it out of her," Jess begged.

"Why would she slip up again and tell you? She can't be that dumb."

Jess laughed, "She might be."

Jay started the car. "Aight. You better come back to me with some good info. Otherwise, we back out here." He drove off.

"Trust me, I'm going to get her to talk one way or another," Jess said confidently.

The next morning, Jasmine got to work and sat down at her desk. She turned on her computer and put her purse in her bottom drawer. Once her computer powered up, she opened her email and looked at her calendar. She had a 9:30 meeting and an on-air story at 10:15. She pulled out her notebook and flipped it open to a blank page. Her email caught her eye as a new one popped up in bold from her manager.

Jasmine, please see me in my office, now.

She dropped her notebook and got up and walked over to her manager's office. He sat in his seat with his glasses on, looking at photos on his desk. She walked in smiling, greeted him, then took a seat. Her eyes were drawn down to the photos on his desk and at first, she couldn't see what they were; her view was upside down.

"Jasmine, I really hate to have this conversation. You are a great asset here and your ratings are great. However, when we had our team at a crime site last night, we were shocked to see you in the photos," he said and slid the photos down in front of her.

Jasmine looked down and picked them up one by one and examined the images. They showed Fox and her walking into the house last night, hand in hand. She looked them over and slowly laid them back on the desk. Her hands became instantly sweaty, leaving small smudges of sweat on the photos.

"I...I don't understand," Jasmine replied.

"I can't have someone representing our brand, our network, our image, and be associated with criminals."

"What criminals? We were not arrested. We didn't do anything wrong. We just went to a party!" Jasmine defended herself.

"A party that was raided for drugs and guns. We were tipped off on the police scanner and showed up just in time to catch you walking in there."

Jasmine sucked her teeth and shifted in her seat uncomfortably. "I have never been arrested. I am not a criminal."

"I'm sorry, we have to let you go."

"This is crazy." Jasmine stood up. "I didn't even do anything wrong."

Not having the words to fix things, Jasmine stormed out of the office and back to her desk. Everyone in the office knew what happened and watched her as she packed her belongings from her desk. She didn't have much because she just started there not too long ago. She shoved everything she could in her purse and looked up to see the office members quietly staring at her.

"Fuck y'all looking at?" she questioned out loud and walked out.

When she got to her car, she broke down. Her anger turned to sadness as the reality sat in that she was fired from her dream job. How would she explain it to her next employer? How would she pay her bills? What would she do about getting another job? How long would it take? How hard would it be? Her mind raced all over as she started the car and headed home. She wanted nothing but to just lay in bed with a pint of ice cream and her feelings.

Chapter 8

The Set Up

I woke up, confused and torn. I was always a man of
many sides, but I never experienced this feeling before. I rolled
over and saw Jasmine up, getting dressed, and I just watched
her. I felt so good knowing she was mine. She was making me
complete and happy and I never felt this way before. I also
never fully placed this much trust in anyone before, not even
my boys. I trusted them, but I would never fully put my guard
down, so when it came to Jasmine, I was conflicted. My heart
wanted to trust her and believe that she was feeling the same
way as me, but how could I trust her when I got robbed right
after she found out about my stash spot. It was such a huge
coincidence. Even though she said she had nothing to do with it
and she is the epitome of a good girl, I couldn't help but
question her loyalty.

I was pissed at myself for even getting this deep in my
feelings for the damn girl to even have these issues. I was the
king of fucking and moving on to the next. I don't know what
happened here or how I even got to this point. It fucks with my
mind, but then this little spot in my heart just takes over and
makes me feel all warm and gushy and shit. I didn't even know
who I was anymore.

After Jasmine left, I got up and went to see Rev. He
would be released in two days and I had everything set up for
his welcome home party at my crib. I had tons of liquor, weed,
friends and music. That's all we needed. Rev would be happy

with just a blunt and a bottle of Henny. He was simple, but I wanted to make sure it was a dope party for Rev and Jasmine.

My plan was to also introduce Jasmine to my boys at this party. She was becoming such an integrated part of my life, it was only right. It was her birthday, so it was the perfect time to bring everyone together. I decided today I would go pick out some birthday gifts for her. I know she just lost her job, so I decided to give her cash and a couple pairs of shoes. You could never go wrong with shoes and money.

After returning from the mall, I stopped by to catch up with Joey and Chuck. They were at the pool hall, betting on a game, like always. Joey was losing as usual, but he talked the most shit. I never even wasted my time betting because Chuck was always the winner in pool; it was his game.

"Why don't you just stop betting? You know you gonna lose," I said to Joey.

"Nah, I'm still in this. I can still beat him," Joey argued.

I sucked my teeth and shook my head. "Look, I gotta figure out the truth about Jasmine," I changed the subject.

"What truth?" Chuck questioned.

"I just want to know if she real. Like can I trust her? Is she really down for me or the quick money?"

"That's easy," Joey said and hit the ball and missed the pocket entirely.

"How is that easy?" I was confused.

"It is. Just set the bitch up," Joey said and stood up straight, leaning his pool stick against the bar. "Look, all you gotta do is see if she would snitch on you."

"What you mean?" I was all ears.

"Let's say someone wanted to get info out of her about you or someone wanted to set you up. If she helps them to save herself, then she a snitch bitch and you know what to do from there."

"Man, I ain't about to set that damn girl up to where she gotta choose herself or me," I replied.

"Look, you got a lot of bread to just be fucking with some bitch who ain't about this life. She can't be no punk ass scary bitch," Joey explained.

"You right. I think I got this, though. I'm already on it."

"I know I'm right," Joey smirked.

"Don't do nothing stupid, just keep her around. You know true loyalty reveals itself in time," Chuck added.

"I ain't got time," I replied and shook my head. Chuck sucked his teeth and went back to his game.

I finished the conversation and watched them play the rest of their game, then headed home. I was in dire need of some pussy. I had been so stressed out lately I haven't even had the time or right mindset to fuck. I was horny and wanted to slide right in it as soon as I got home. Jasmine was walking around the house in some little pink boy shorts, so half her ass was hanging out. My dick was hard as soon as I walked in the door and saw her. I grabbed her by the arm and led her into the bedroom and fucked her so good she cried. I thought that shit was weird, but she nutted so hard that she laid there and cried. It must have been good for her, I guess.

After sex, I rolled a blunt up and told her I was hungry. There wasn't anything in the house to cook, so I sent her to the store to get some stuff. I also had a taste for cookies and sweet shit. I had the munchies because after I fucked her soul out and rolled the blunt, I smoked the entire thing. She threw on some sweat pants and ran out for me.

When she got out the car, she jogged across the store and got what she needed. When she walked out the store, there were two men standing on both sides of the door with masks on. They grabbed her from each side and one placed his gloved hand over her mouth. They dragged her now kicking and squirming body to a truck, threw her inside and got in with her.

One of them held her down, while the other tied her wrists together and tied a blindfold over her eyes. She squirmed and tried to scream for help as the third accomplice drove off to an unknown destination. Her screams were muffled by the gloved hand over her mouth, which made it nearly impossible to make any noise loud enough for anyone to hear outside of the truck.

After a short ride, they yanked her out the car and led her to an abandoned house. She still couldn't see anything, but smelled an old mildew smell. She was shoved to the ground where she fell to her hands and knees. Her screams were useless as they quickly stuffed something in her mouth. She worked tirelessly to spit it out, with no success.

"Look, stop trying to scream, it ain't going to help you," a voice spoke up. She stopped moving and turned towards the voice. "Stop screaming and I'll take the gag out your mouth. Understand?"

Jasmine shook her head yes and sniffled. She wanted to wipe the tears rolling down her face, but had no available hands. She reached her shoulders and arms up and tried to wipe her face on her sleeve. Half way successful and half way unsuccessful, she still had a half wet face. The guy reached over and pulled the gag out of her mouth.

"We won't hurt you. Relax. As long as you help us with what we want, you're good. See, we know you're Fox's girlfriend. We want him, and you're going to help us get him."

"What do you need me for? I don't have anything to do with this!" she complained.

"All you need to do is help us get to his money. He doesn't have to know it's you. He doesn't have to know anything. In a good faith effort on our part, if you get us to the money, we will hit you off with a check."

"I don't know where his money is," she whined.

"You lying," the other voice spoke up. "You know where it is and I know you want this check. Stop playing."

"I don't know. He doesn't tell me that stuff!"

"Listen, we aren't going to play this game with you. You got forty-eight hours to find out where he keeps his money and get me that info."

"He is not going to tell me! How do I just ask him without him knowing what is going on!"

"Forty-eight hours. Give me the location or bad things will start to happen. One by one. You don't even want to know what those bad things are," the first voice answered.

"Really bad things," the second voice chimed in.

"You get me the info and write down the address. Leave it in an envelope and leave it in the phone booth in front of 3rd and Broad Street by 6 p.m. tomorrow."

"I don't know the location," she continued to plead.

"I don't give a fuck. Find out because I know where to find you and your family."

She cried more tears and sniffled as the voices stopped talking. Her mind raced as she thought about all the options. She really didn't have any. Risking her friends and family life

114

was not an option. If she told Fox about it, she still had forty-eight hours to get the location or else she still risked her friends and family. Catch 22, she thought.

Once she realized the voices had trailed off and left, she sat quietly, listening for any noise that could clue into where they were. Finally, after about thirty minutes, she realized they were gone and probably were not coming back. It was complete silence as she tried to get her hands untied first. After many attempts to break free, she couldn't get it and reached up with both tied hands and used her wrist to push her blindfold up. It was tight, so it hurt her eyes, but she finally got it up enough to be able to raise her head and look underneath it. Her eyes darted around the room, taking in her surroundings. It looked like an abandoned house with no furniture, and certainly didn't look to be in livable condition. She wiggled up to her feet, ran to the door and out to the street. She didn't recognize the neighborhood at all, but figured she couldn't be too far. The drive didn't seem like it was that long. As she ran, she used her hands to push up her blindfold more and more until it was completely off. She still couldn't get her hands free, but continued to run until she came to a corner store, where she went directly to the cashier and begged her to untie her hands. Immediately after being free from the bondage, she took off running until she came across a subway station, where she managed to make her way back to her car. Afraid and confused on what to do about the whole situation, she went by Jess' apartment to talk.

As soon as Jess saw her, she knew something was wrong. She grabbed her, sat down on the couch and dried her tears for her. Jasmine was crying uncontrollably and couldn't even get the words out to tell her what happened.

115

"What happened now?" Jess said as Jasmine laid on her chest and she stroked her hair.

"Some guys just grabbed me up," Jasmine sobbed.

"What? Who? Talk to me," Jess demanded.

"I don't know. They blindfolded me and threatened me."

"What did they want? What happened?" Jess asked, anxiously waiting on answers.

"They just grabbed me and took me to an empty house. They wanted his money!"

"Are you kidding me? Why would you have it?"

"They wanted to know where he keeps his money."

"Did you tell them?" Jess asked.

"No, of course not. I can't do that to him."

"Girl! How did they let you go?"

"They said I have forty-eight hours to get them the location of his money or bad things are going to happen to my family and friends."

"Wait. What? Forty-eight hours? What type of shit is that?"

"Yeah, I don't know what to do. Should I tell him?" Jasmine sat up.

"Fuck no. What good is that going to do? You tell him and then you don't tell these guys where it is and bad shit is going to start happening!"

"But I can't tell them where it is at. I promised not tell anyone."

"So you know where it is?"

"Yea, he told me recently, but it's for emergencies only."

"Wait a second. He just told you recently where he keeps his money and all of a sudden you get snatched up by some random guys and given forty-eight hours to come up with the location?" Jess said as she jumped up.

"Yea." Jasmine looked up, confused.

"Man, this don't smell right. This a setup. Where he say he keep it?"

"But why doesn't that make sense?" Jasmine said, ignoring her question.

"No real nigga trying to get a location is going to give you forty-eight hours to one, disappear, two, go to the cops, or three, tell the nigga they are trying to rob him!" Jess exclaimed.

"I guess. But why would he do this? This doesn't make any sense."

"I don't know, baby girl, but I do smell bullshit. You need to leave that nigga. He playing games. You just got fired because of his dumb ass. He beat your ass and now he playing games with you." Jess caught an attitude.

"No, don't be like that. There has to be another explanation. There has to be," Jasmine pleaded.

"Tell them where it is then. I bet money it's fake and he just wants to see if you will snitch. Tell them exactly where it is. Fuck with his head since he wanna fuck with yours."

"But what if it's not him?" Jasmine got frustrated.

"It is him. You need to leave him. Tell them where it is at and just disappear. You know it's a game, so fuck it. Tell them and let him know you're not stupid and you know what's up, then leave him alone. You need to worry about your safety. He's crazy!"

117

"You're right, though. Like this is too much and I can't handle this. My life is a fucking mess right now," Jasmine complained.

"Get out now before it gets too late. Move out of town. Nothing is keeping you here now. You don't have a job here anymore. You're done with school and you need to leave that man. I told you this from the minute you told me you met a dope boy. All they do is come in and fuck shit up and leave."

Chapter 9

Meet the Family

I made sure I woke up early enough to get shit done before the party. I told Jasmine not to worry about helping out since it was her birthday, so I sent her to a spa for the day to get a massage and a facial, then get her nails and toes done. I had a thing for white nails, so I made my request. She was with it. Something about a pretty manicured hand with white nails wrapped around my dick turned me on. I planned to get that visual later.

My cousin cooked all the food for the party and I gave her a couple hundred for her troubles. She had it looking like Thanksgiving with everything from fried chicken, collard greens, mac and cheese, yams, rice, and a variety of desserts. She even hooked up an adult punch. Of course, I had bottles of Henny, Cîroc and Coronas in the cooler also. I was more than prepared to show Rev a good time.

Rev was more than excited to come hang out. He was feeling a lot better and missed hanging out with his friends, getting bitches, and getting money. He did mention he couldn't drink liquor because he was still taking antibiotics for an infection he developed on his wound. It was all good; I knew he would hit the blunt instead.

Chuck and Joey were out already handling some business, but were going to pick up Rev for me at 9 tonight. I promised Rev that tomorrow I would get him that work he wanted so he could get himself back on his feet as soon as possible and take care of his bills and family. I had to go meet up with my connect to get the order and he was all the way on the other side of town. After I checked on my cousin and the food, I headed out to make that run.

I got in my car, jumped on the highway and turned my radio up. I zoned out and drove until my phone rang. I saw the name, turned the music down and hit accept, as I tried to concentrate on the road. My connect said he had an emergency and would have to link up with me at 4 p.m. today instead. I was pissed because I was already in my car and on the way, but there was nothing I could do about it. I hit the first U-turn I could and headed back home. I was up early with nothing to do now since Jasmine was out at the spa. She was supposed to be leaving by 3:30, so I had all day to bullshit until it was time to link up with the boys for the party.

I smoked a blunt and fell asleep, but woke up when my cousin came in the room saying she was done cooking. She grabbed the money off the dresser and headed out, saying she would be back later for the party. I rolled out of bed and went to fix myself a plate. I couldn't wait for tonight because the smell was invading my nose all the way from downstairs in the kitchen. It was calling me and I have no self-control at all. After eating, I checked my phone and saw that Chuck called me. Of course, he wanted me to come help him with business and since my plans got postponed, I really had no excuse not to, so I headed out to link up with him.

We spent the rest of the day breaking down product and bagging it. It was time to make some money in the next few weeks. We were planning to make a major come up and were excited to have Rev back on the team. It was time to grind. It was closing in on 3:30 and I didn't even realize it. We still had a ton more to do and I didn't want to leave Chuck and Joey to do it alone.

I pulled my phone out and called Jasmine. "Babe."

"What's up?" she answered.

"You done at the spa?" I asked.

"Yea, I'm actually headed out to the lobby to leave a tip now."

"Can you pick something up for me?"

"Yea. What you need?"

"I'll text you the address and I'll let him know you are coming."

"Ok, but what is it?" she inquired.

"It just Rev's welcome home gift."

"Oh ok. Cool, just send me the address."

We hung up and I sent the address to her phone. I called up my connect and told him a woman named Jasmine would be picking up the work instead of me. The money was already in a secured location, waiting for him as soon as he delivered the product. We had a good relationship and the trust between us had grown over the years. He knew I was a man of my word, as I know he is a man of his word. If I ever tried to screw him over, I would be dead before I could even try to run. We had a mutual understanding and respect for one another.

When I hung the phone up, Joey and Chuck were staring at me like they saw a ghost. I slid my phone into my pocket and continued bagging the work. They continued to stare at me, expecting me to say something.

"Nigga...so you sending ya girl to pick your work up now?" Joey asked, already knowing the answer.

"Yea, why not?" I asked seriously.

"Aw shit. Fox must be in love because when has he ever trusted anyone with his work?" Chuck clapped his hands and laughed.

"All she gotta do is pick it up and go straight home with it. It ain't 'bout shit. Chill out," I defended myself.

"Ok. If you say so. Better hope she don't go missing on your ass," Joey teased.

"Nah. She wouldn't even know what to do with that shit," I explained.

When we finally finished, it was going on 8 p.m. and I figured we should go pick up Rev, bring him by the house, and get an early start because everyone was hungry after I told them about the food my cousin cooked. We cleaned, picked Rev up and went back to my house.

I walked in the crib and could still smell the food. I went straight to the kitchen and warmed up plate two while the rest of them followed behind me. The DJ came through and set up quickly and had music playing in no time. Jasmine was upstairs getting dressed in something cute and comfortable since we weren't going out. I still told her to look nice since she would be meeting all of my boys.

When she came downstairs, I was one hundred percent satisfied with how beautiful she looked. I was proud to show her off. She had on ripped black jeans that hugged her hips and ass so perfectly, a white tank top and a pair of Giuseppe sneakers I recently bought her. Her lips wore a bright red lipstick that made me want to fuck the shit out of her mouth. She walked in the room and confidently joined me and my boys.

"Aye, this my girl, Jasmine," I said with a smile.

They all smiled, shook her hand and Rev gave her a hug. I could tell they were genuinely happy for me to be happy, so they accepted her with wide open arms. Chuck was the mature one out of us, so I knew he would hold any comments and opinions until in private. Joey joked a lot about never trusted bitches, but I knew deep down inside he wanted to. Rev was the cool one and he just went with the flow and minded his business. Jasmine greeted everyone and went to fix a plate. She checked on everyone first to make sure they had everything they needed, then sat down to eat her food. I watched her and admired how fly she was.

"Oh yeah, babe, you picked that up, right? Where is it?" I asked, remembering that I sent her to get my work for me.

"It is still in my trunk. You need it?"

"No, don't worry about it. I'll get it out in the morning."

The next hour was filled with more people arriving and more meet and greets for Jasmine. Everyone who came was a close friend of mine, someone I respected or someone I trusted. The food was good, the drinks were good and the company was good. I felt like I could relax in my own home with all parts of my circle as one. I felt good about my situation. My girl and my family and friends all on one accord.

Soon, one by one, Jasmine's friends started to show up. Finally, some ladies to keep my boys entertained, I thought. I ain't want my girl to be walking around like the only piece of meat for these savages. I know they knew their boundaries, but I wanted them to have something else to look at. Everyone was mingling and having a good time, so I went to the hall closet and pulled out her gifts.

"Happy birthday, babe," I said as I crept up behind her and handed her the bags.

A huge smile formed on her face as she grabbed the bags and dug inside. She pulled out the gifts and admired her new designer things. She was still not used to buying things of this quality and it felt good to be able to give them to her.

"Thank you! These are dope. I like them all." Jasmine put the bags down and planted three kisses all over my face. I grabbed her ass and pulled her closer to my body.

"Oh, so you going to do that in front of everyone?" she giggled.

"Yea, you got a problem?" I asked and pulled her even closer.

The doorbell rang and interrupted us before it got any freakier in the hallway. Jasmine pulled away and smiled as she walked to the front door and opened it. Her best friend hugged her and walked in with an enormous smile. They quickly made their way to the kitchen so she could get a drink.

"Jess, I know you're hungry," Jasmine said as she handed her a red cup of punch.

"Nah. I actually ate not too long ago," Jess said and pouted.

"Oh ok. Well, there's a ton of food here if you do get hungry. Come meet everyone."

The two girls walked up to the hallway to find Fox, but the only thing left there were her gifts. She grabbed them and ran them upstairs to the bedroom for safe keeping, then headed back downstairs. She scanned the room and saw Fox, then grabbed Jess' hand to pull her towards him.

"Hey, babe. This is Jess, my old roommate." Jasmine pointed to her friend.

"Hey, what's up?" Fox replied.

"Nice party," Jess said over the music.

"Thanks. There's food and drinks all over. Help yourself."

"Ok," Jess smiled and Jasmine grabbed her hand and pulled her away.

"Come meet his friends," Jasmine gushed.

"Any cute ones?"

"Um…kinda." They both laughed.

The rest of the guys sat in the living room, drinking, joking and playing spades. They didn't even realize the new girls who came in the house. Jasmine looked around and said 'Fuck it.' Too many people, too many introductions and interruptions.

"It's too many of them," Jasmine said to Jess.

"It's all good, I'll meet them later." Jess blew it off. Before she could turn and take a sip of her drink, her eyes narrowed in on Rev. Her heart stopped and she froze. Her mind raced back to that fateful night she would never be the same. Everything in her body turned cold as she stared at his face. That's that nigga, she thought to herself. Everything suddenly made sense and she couldn't believe it.

Jess caught herself staring and quickly put her head down, then walked to the kitchen. She leaned on the counter and tried to calm herself down. Her chest heaved up and down as she tried to compose herself. Jasmine followed in behind her and looked at her, concerned.

"Are you ok?" Jasmine asked.

"Yea…yea, I am," Jess answered. "I just got like a random hot flash. I'm ok."

"Ok, old lady," Jasmine joked. "You want some water?"

"Nah, I'm good. I'm not really feeling good," Jess lied. "I should go home and lay down."

"Aw, you just got here, Jess!" Jasmine whined.

"I know, but I don't feel good."

"Well, you can lay down upstairs in our bed. I don't want you to leave yet."

"I really don't wanna be in y'all personal space." Jess tried to lie her way out of it.

"No, it's ok. I want you to stay. Please stay," Jasmine begged.

"Ok, I'll go lay down. Maybe I just need to take a nap."

"Ok! I won't bother you. Just take some water." Jasmine got excited she was staying and grabbed her a water bottle out of the fridge. She walked her upstairs and let her in the bedroom. After making sure she was ok, she walked out and closed the bedroom door behind her to head back down to the party.

Jess laid there, faking sick, staring at the ceiling. She laid there and connected all the dots, but still couldn't make sense of it. The nigga she shot was downstairs, alive and well. Would he recognize her and if he did, would he say anything? Jess was confused on how to play it. She feared for her life actually.

She pulled out her cell and began to text Jay and tell him she was in the same house as the nigga she shot. Before she could finish the text, Rev walked into the room and quietly closed the door behind him and locked it. Jess sat up quickly and went cold again. Her heartbeat five times faster than normal, as he walked over to her slowly. Once he got to the bedside, he hovered above her and said nothing.

The fear in her paralyzed her vocal cords because she didn't even say a word. He stared maniacally down at her, wanting to crack her skull in after what she did to him. His mind drifted back to the cold metal that was held up against his head; the fear of never seeing his friends or family again. The lack of value of his life made him sick to his stomach as he looked down at her in disgust.

His large hands suddenly wrapped around her neck as she gasped for breath to no avail. The soul began to drain from her eyes as she kicked and kicked to be released. She slowly mouthed please, as no sound came out. In that moment, he realized he couldn't kill her; not like that. Not in my house in my bed with all of our friends and family around. He let go quickly and she gasped in all the air she could as fast as she could, repeatedly, until the pressure in her head returned to normal. Her heartbeat slowed down and her complexion went back to normal.

"Please don't kill me," she whimpered out as she grabbed her own neck to massage the pain she felt around her throat from his fingers digging deep into it.

"Bitch, you shot me. You almost killed me," he angrily said as he paced back and forth, trying to calm himself down. "How the fuck do you know Fox? Who are you?"

Jess said nothing. She gripped her cell phone and slowly pulled herself up so she was sitting on the bed instead of laying. He stopped pacing and stared at her. His eyes quickly scanned the room and saw her purse. He ran to it, grabbed it and emptied its contents on the floor. He rummaged through them and threw it down, content that there was no weapon.

"How do you know Fox?" he asked again more sternly.

"I don't. I know Jasmine," she finally spoke. "You know Bop? He was my boyfriend and you put him in jail. Your big fucking mouth. I know what you're doing. You a rat! I bet Fox don't know you a rat, do he?"

Rev stopped in his tracks; it finally made sense to him. He thought back to that night and remembered what she said to him: something about snitches. She knew. She knew what he thought nobody knew. He leaned back over her, towering above her small frame once again.

"The only way you live is if you keep your mouth shut," he grabbed her face. "You say a word and you die." He threw her face down and she slammed down on the bed. He began to walk towards the door.

She didn't know what to say, so she said nothing. She didn't want to die and didn't know how Rev was going to react to anything she said at this point. This was the first time she let her fear overcome her and it shook her to her core. Anything she said would trigger him.

"If I say something, you know you are over with? If I don't say anything, I'm over with," Jess sat up straight. "At this point, I'm fucked."

Rev stopped and turned to look at her. "If you say anything, you die." He continued to walk to the door and unlocked it. "That is your warning. Remember you said it, snitches get stitches." He left the room.

Jess exhaled and fell back onto the bed, relaxing her tense muscles. She laid there a moment, replaying everything that had just happened in her head. The pieces of the puzzle all started making sense. All this time she did not know that Jasmine's boyfriend was in business with the rat! She picked up her cell phone and started texting Jay about what happened, but was interrupted when Jasmine walked in the room.

"Uhuh...I saw Rev come up here, what he want? I know he was trying to get your number." Jasmine giggled.

"Oh yeah, girl, he wanted it," Jess lied.

"He is cute, but I think he has a girl," Jasmine slurred slightly. The drinks were starting to get to her.

"Oh damn. Figures." Jess pretended to care.

Jasmine plopped down on the bed next to Jess, "I made up my mind."

"About what?"

"I'm going to say something to Fox about them people grabbing me up for his location. It has to be him testing me."

"I told you," Jess replied nonchalantly. Her mind wasn't in it right now. She gave zero fucks about Fox testing Jasmine and her bullshit, she just wanted to go the fuck home and talk to Jay. She wanted to feel safe and currently, she felt nowhere near it.

"I'll tell him tomorrow," Jasmine tried to say without slurring her words.

Chapter 10

Nobody was Ever Real

    Jasmine rolled over and squinted her eyes at the sunlight that peeked through the curtains; it immediately hurt her eyes and head. She moaned in disgust at the taste of liquor still on her stale breath. Her body felt like she got hit by a Mack truck…twice. It took all of her energy to fully open her eyes and focus and she saw Fox sprawled out on the bed next to her, fully clothed, with sneakers still on. She, on the other hand, was butt ass naked with a full face of makeup smeared all over her face.

    She got up slowly and walked to the bathroom where she literally fell onto the toilet and peed. When she got up, she turned her nose up at the pure alcohol she just pissed out her system. She reached over and turned the shower on hot and stuck her hand in, waiting for it to warm up. Once it was to her liking, she pulled her hair back in a bun and wrapped it up in a scarf that lay on the bathroom vanity.

    The shower felt like God's hands washing away the dirt, as she struggled to keep her composure and not vomit all the toxins she ingested the night before. Once she finished up her shower, she stepped out, wrapped a towel around her body and walked back out to Fox. She gently removed his sneakers and pushed his legs onto the bed all the way. She pulled the blanket up over him, trying not to wake him, but he felt the light touches and woke up.

    "Morning," Fox said as he opened his eyes.

"Good morning, babe," Jasmine replied and leaned down and kissed him on the forehead.

"How you feel? You was tore up last night. After Jess left, you started taking shots to the head," he laughed.

"I don't even remember her leaving, and damn sure don't remember taking shots!" Jasmine sat on the bed next to him.

"Look, Fox, I gotta talk to you about something," Jasmine said and stared at him.

"What's up?" He ran his hands across her still damp thighs.

"Did you try to set me up?" Jasmine asked flatly.

"Huh? What you mean?" Fox was confused and sat up on the bed.

"Did you send some people to test me? To find out where you keep your money?"

"What? Hell no." Fox stared at her in confusion. "Why would I do that? Fuck is you talking about?"

"Someone snatched me up yesterday and threatened me. They said I had to tell them where you keep your money."

"Why would you think it was me?" Fox was pissed.

"I don't know. It just seemed fake."

"This ain't no game out here. Why didn't you tell me?"

"I thought it was you testing me since you just told me where it was and then all of a sudden, someone's asking me where it is the next day."

"You need to carry one of my guns." Fox got up and went into his closet. He pulled out a gun and handed it to her. She didn't take it.

"I don't want that," she whined.

131

"Oh, you rather end up in a coma like Rev? It's not a fucking game out here!" Fox yelled at her.

She flinched and took the gun slowly and put it on the bed beside her. He kneeled down in between her legs on the floor and grabbed her hands and kissed them a couple times. Tears began to roll down her face as she realized she was in way over her head.

"What am I supposed to do?" Jasmine sobbed.

"I won't let anything happen to you. Just keep your mouth shut and keep this gun on you. We can go practice at the range this weekend so you're comfortable with it. Don't worry." Fox comforted her.

"Ok, babe." She sniffled and kissed him again on the forehead. She still wasn't one hundred percent convinced he had nothing to do with it, but if he did, then she sure passed his test.

"But get ya butt dressed, I'm taking you to breakfast," Fox smiled and stood up, then headed to the bathroom.

Philadelphia Police Station...

Rev paced back and forth with his hands gripping one another tightly in front of him. Small sweat beads formed on his hairline and slowly trickled down his face. His heart rate was abnormally fast and his breathing was deep and heavy. He tried to remain calm, but his nerves were getting the best of him as he waited.

Detective Johnson walked into the room and closed the door behind him, "What can I do for you, Rev?"

"Man, I gotta get this over with. The nigga Bop's girlfriend knows I set him up. She knows. She is going to blow my cover," Rev blurted out.

"Ok, ok, calm down," Johnson said, motioning for Rev to take a seat and they both sat down. "So she knows. What makes you think she is going to say anything?"

"She is best friends with Fox's girlfriend. She knows I sent Bop away, so she's probably gonna warn Fox!" Rex explained.

"Oh. Ok, I see what you're saying now."

"Yeah, do you see! I gotta get this done with. I gotta get out of here. If Fox finds out, then I'm dead before I even have a chance."

"Ok, calm down, we will figure it out. What we don't want to happen is for her to say anything and ruin all that we worked for. We also don't want you to disappear because that is the worst case scenario for you."

"So what y'all going to do?" Rev questioned.

"Hold tight, son," Johnson said with a smile and lightly pushed Rev on the arm.

"Hold tight? What am I supposed to do?" Rev got angry.

"Let us handle it," Johnson said and stood up.

"He's supposed to meet me today to give me those drugs I asked for," Rev blurted out.

"Oh yea? When were you going to tell us?" Johnson inquired.

"I'm telling you now." Rev looked down. "I asked him for them and he said he would get me some to sell when I got out the hospital. I saw him yesterday and he promised me them, but he was so drunk and with his girl that I just left. I spoke to him this morning and he said he would get them to me today."

"Where? When?" Johnson asked.

133

"I don't know; I didn't ask yet."

"Well, ask and we will be in place. You can finish your part. Last arrest and you're done."

Rev sat there disgusted at himself; he sat for a moment, thinking. What did he get himself into? Giving up his best friend since childhood, a man he considered family. For what? His own freedom? What good was it in a remote location with no family or friends. He was sick. Finally coming to the conclusion that he was fucked and there was nothing he could do, he got up and left the station.

After breakfast, Fox got a call to handle some business, so he dropped Jasmine back off at the house and headed back out. She got inside and locked the door behind her and set the alarm. She slowly walked upstairs and went into the bedroom. She fell into the bed and stretched out and let her guard down. In moments, she was asleep, but was awakened by her cell phone buzzing next to her head on the bed.

"Hey, girl," Jasmine answered.

"You sleep?" Jess questioned after hearing the tiredness in her voice.

"Yea, I was taking a nap."

"Oh, I guess you made your decision on not telling them people about Fox's money?" Jess laughed.

"Girl, I don't know. Fox said it wasn't him, but I am not about to go snitch on his money, so I guess we will see."

"You crazy. Fuck that. I would be out there singing like a bird. I hope you safe, girl."

"I'm good. I can't snitch on him like that. I just can't do it."

"You loyal, I get it, just be careful," Jess warned.

"You were the one saying it's probably just him!"

"Right, but I wanted you to snitch. That's the safest thing. If it is him, you tell the location, but you say 'I know you Fox's people', so you at least cover your tracks. If it is not him and you tell the location, then you just saved a family member's life maybe. You have to choose," Jess explained.

"So you think I should tell them?" Jasmine frowned.

"Duh. I've said this multiple times. Not saying anything doesn't do anything. Fox thinks you loyal now. Ok, and? He should have thought that to begin with. Fuck him."

"I know, I know," Jasmine rolled her eyes.

"So what you about to do today? Sleep?" Jess asked.

"I'm hungover. I need some water and there is nothing left in this house but alcohol. I'm about to run to the store as soon as I get the energy to get up."

"Ok. Well, I was just checking on you. Hit me later." Jess hung up.

Jasmine rolled over and stretched, then closed her eyes again. She wanted water, but her body wouldn't let her move. In minutes, she drifted back to sleep, but woke up quickly. She needed that water, so she dragged her body out the bed and pulled on a pair of sneakers. She set the alarm, left the house and got into her car, then headed to the store.

Fox was finishing up his business when Rev called him and asked about the work that he had for him. He said to meet him at the usual bar where they meet up and play pool at. It was a local corner bar and the owners were good friends with Fox, so they didn't mind him being there. They turned a blind eye to any drug transactions, as long as Fox gave them hush money sporadically. Rev arrived first and waited for him. He ordered a Henny and Coke to ease his nerves. He had already alerted the police to the time and location, but didn't see them anywhere, but he knew they were there or somewhere close.

Fox arrived and sat on the stool next to Rev and ordered a shot of Patron with lime juice. He wasn't feeling like himself after all that drinking he did the night before, but the habit of drinking when there was a bar around was strong. He paid with a twenty-dollar bill and told the bartender to keep the change. The two of them talked about the party and everything that was going on there.

Two men walked in and sat at the bar next to them. Rev looked over at them nonchalantly; he knew they were probably undercover. Fox continued to talk it up about the party. He asked Rev what he thought about Jasmine and Rev said all positive things and bigged up his ego. He let him know he had a good one; she was bad. Fox smiled at his friend's approval. The two men sitting next to them never ordered a drink and Fox noticed. He began to watch them and wondered what they were there for, if not to drink.

"Let me make a phone call real quick," Fox said and walked towards the door to get away from the noise. He put his phone to his ear and listened to it ring as he made his way towards his car. "Cancel that. Meet me at the crib."

"Ok babe," Jasmine said.

The two men got up and followed him towards the door and outside. He turned and saw them approaching as he ended the call on his phone. He knew it was definitely something up and put the phone in his pocket and laid his hand on his gun in preparation.

"Philadelphia Police," one shouted and showed his badge on his waist clip as they both raised their guns. "Don't move."

Fox stood there frozen. He wanted to run so bad, but knew he wouldn't get anywhere and possibly a bullet in the back. Deciding to cooperate, he raised his arms to surrender. One cop reached into his pocket and pulled out his handcuffs and grabbed Fox's arms one by one and cuffed them together.

"You have the right to remain silent…" the officer began to read him his rights as he walked him outside to the eight awaiting cop cars, marked and unmarked. Fox had no idea this was going down. Rev sat at the bar watching; not a word said and he didn't move. He stood up and began to walk towards the door. Fox looked back and saw Rev standing there alone outside in front of the bar. No police had cuffed him or approached him yet. Fox turned back repeatedly and still saw no cuffs.

Jasmine grabbed the bottle of water out of the large refrigerator in the store and started to walk towards the cashier, but turned back and grabbed a second one. When she got to the counter to pay, she pulled a ten-dollar bill out of her purse and handed it to the cashier. He returned her change and she grabbed the bottles, then left the store. As soon as she walked out, two sets of hands grabbed her while one hand was placed over her mouth. They dragged her to a truck where they tried to push her inside. This time, she wasn't going down without a fight. Her feet were flinging all over the place as she struggled to get loose. Her feet landed in the chest of one of them a few times and it caused him to stumble back, which gave her the opportunity to be in the grip of one man instead of two for a moment. She vigorously fought her way out of his arms and was able to pull her gun out of her purse. She never shot a gun and was scared as hell, but the need to survive was much greater. She knew these were the same people looking for

Fox's money. She pulled the safety back and pulled the trigger once and the two men scrambled down low to avoid the bullets. She shot off another and they retreated to the truck without her. She ran the opposite way to her car and hopped in and sped off like she never did before. Her hands were shaking as she tried to catch her breath. Her mind raced as she tried to think quickly about what to do. She pulled out some tissue from her purse and began to rub the gun all over, wiping her prints off. She didn't think she hit anyone, but she wasn't taking any chances. After cleaning the gun while driving 85mph, she tossed it out the window in a swamp area nearby. Finally calming down and catching her breath, she reached over to look for her cell phone in her purse. She called Fox and got no answer, so she sped up to head home to get to him. After a few miles, she flew by a police officer who immediately turned his sirens on and hit a U-turn to follow her. "Fuck!" Jasmine screamed.

The cop pulled her over and she sat nervously, waiting for them to approach her car. She took deep breaths to relax and not appear nervous. It wasn't working, she was terrified and it showed. An officer stepped out of his car, hand on hip and approached her driver's side.

"Ma'am, do you realize you were going 90mph in a 65?" he questioned.

"No. I didn't."

"You didn't know you were going that fast? Are you in a rush?"

"Yea, I was just trying to get home to meet my boyfriend."

"Is there an emergency?"

"No."

"License and registration, ma'am."

The officer peered in her backseat and checked her car out. Jasmine reached over and pulled her documents out of the glove compartment and her wallet, then handed them to her. She stared straight ahead, scared that the fear in her eyes would show.

"Are you ok, ma'am?" The officer grew suspicious of her nervous demeanor.

"Yea, I'm ok," she replied and forced a smile.

"Ok. I'll be right back." The officer took her documents to his car.

After running her documents, he saw her record came back clean, with no warrants, but there was an alert for her model car and color. Apparently, it was seen nearby a shooting. He immediately had a suspicion she was involved and called for backup. Jasmine called Fox again and still no answer. She was getting nervous as she waited and waited. She looked out her rearview mirror and saw two more cop cars pull up. Her heart sank as she watched them exit their cars and begin to approach her car, hands on guns, ready to draw. She waited patiently for them to get to her.

The same officer approached her car at a distance, with his hand on his gun, still in the holster. "Ma'am, can you go ahead and step out the car for me?"

"Why? What is wrong?" she questioned.

"Just go on and step out the car for me slowly, with hands visible," he responded.

Jasmine opened the door and stepped out with her hands slightly raised. She nervously stood facing the officers and wondered what was going to happen next. She breathed a sigh of relief, thinking about how she threw the gun out of the car just moments earlier. If they stopped her with that, then she would have a felony on her hands.

"We are going to take a look in your car, ma'am," the officer said as he approached closer. "Do you have anything in your car or on you?"

"No, nothing," Jasmine said confidently.

"Ok. I'm going to just lightly pat you down. Raise your hands up and stand with feet apart," the officer said, came over and patted her down quickly and found nothing. "Stand over here for me." He motioned for her to stand by the back of the car.

The other officers opened all of her car doors and began going through all of her belongings in her car from top to bottom, leaving not one space unchecked; they found nothing. One officer reached down on her driver's side and popped the trunk. He walked back and lifted it up and she immediately almost lost her feet from under her when she saw the book bag she picked up for Fox the other day. She completely forgot about it and never opened it to see what it was. The officer unzipped it and laughed as he saw packages of white drugs wrapped in saran wrap in the bag.

"Ma'am, what is in the book bag?" the officer asked.

"I don't know, it's not mine. I never even opened it," she explained.

"It's in your car. You don't know what it is?"

"I have no idea. Someone just asked me to pick something up for them. I had no idea what it was." She tried to explain more.

"It doesn't matter that it is not yours, it is in your car. There is no one else here to claim it," another officer chimed in.

"Please, it's not mine," Jasmine pleaded and began to cry.

On the way to the police station, Jasmine cried like never before. With no free hands to wipe her tears or dripping nose, her shirt was drenched. She tried everything to get out of it; pleading and begging the police to let her go. There was no way they would let her and she knew it. Once inside the holding cell, she cried uncontrollably, realizing what really just happened. She had no idea how much weight she had in her trunk and how serious of a charge it was, but she knew it was going to be bad. On top that, she called Fox twice and got no answer and was getting worried. He is the only one with the money to get her a lawyer and bail her out.

When she finally got a chance to make a phone call, she called Fox again, but still no answer. She was devastated and still crying uncontrollably. The officer didn't see young women in this predicament often and felt a little sorry for her. He let her make another call and this time, she called Jess. She needed to be bailed out immediately and had only one choice.

"Jess, listen to me; I got locked up. I'm going to need to get bailed out. Can you go to Fox's house for me, or get in touch with him? He's not answering his phone," Jasmine blurted out as soon as Jess answered.

"Oh my God, Jazz. Are you ok? But listen, word on the street is Fox got locked up today too."

"What?" Jasmine cried out.

"Yea, I heard he got picked up. I don't know why or what's going on."

"Ok, then I need you to do me a favor. Can you go pick up some of his money for me? I need bail. I can't sit in here. Then I can get him out."

"Yea, of course, anything. Where is it?" Jess asked.

Jasmine hesitated, but didn't know any other option. She was not going to sit in this jail any longer than she needed to. Fox would have to understand; Jess was her best friend that she trusted.

She turned away from the officer and whispered, "Charter school on 5th street. Get in there through the vent on the lower part of the roof. Blue locker, 252. You have to get something to cut the lock. Please don't tell anyone else and just grab what we need to get me out. I'm going to call you back when they set my bail amount. Stay with your phone on."

"Ok. I got you, 252. Be careful. Call me back," Jess said and hung up.

In that moment, Jasmine realized her life was in complete shambles. She lost her job and now she was arrested for possession of drugs that were not even hers. The trust between her and her man was up in the air. Someone was after her safety and her man was now locked up too; it couldn't get any worse. She was ushered back to the holding cell to wait for further instructions. She sat numb from all the bullshit. She was so distraught she couldn't even cry anymore. It was like she was out of tears. Her head ached from the anxiety and stress of what was going to happen next.

Fox sat in a room with a cup of water in front of him. His head hung low as his eyes were closed and he tried to figure out how to work his angles. Obviously, the cops wanted info or answers and didn't have any solid evidence, otherwise, he would have already been charged. He knew the drill and knew the game well. What he didn't understand was why Rev wasn't arrested as well. He is just as much involved in their drug business as he is.

142

When he opened his eyes, he looked around the small, dark room. All of the windows were blocked with shades and the only thing in the room were two other seats at the table he sat at. Patiently, he waited until a detective entered the room with a folder and sat down across from him. They stared at each other silently for a moment, until the detective spoke up.

"Son, let's make this real easy and fast for both our sake," Detective Johnson said.

"I'm not your son," Fox replied with an attitude.

"Ok, FOX. Let's make this easy. We know who you are, what you do and how you do it."

"So why am I in here with you and not in a cell?" Fox interrupted him. "Am I being arrested or questioned because I want my lawyer."

Detective Johnson stared at Fox, realizing this was going to be a difficult one. Fox wasn't going to turn himself in easily. He knew he had the bait, though, so he wasn't worried one bit. "You know we arrested your girlfriend?" Johnson said, ignoring his request for counsel.

Fox's head jerked up. "For what?"

"Well, we have reason to believe she was involved in a shooting."

Fox chuckled, "Come on, that's the best y'all could do? I know she wasn't involved in no damn shooting. That's bullshit and you know it."

"Is it? Well for one, her vehicle was spotted at the scene of the shooting. Witnesses have made statements saying a woman of her exact description was seen fleeing the scene. She was pulled over going 90mph stating that she was rushing home to you, which we know wasn't even home at the time, so is it really bullshit?"

143

"It's all bullshit. You made a story up."

"Why would we?" Detective Johnson asked and leaned back in his chair.

"I don't know. To try to weaken me."

"Weaken you for what?"

"Look, what do you want from me?" Fox got annoyed.

"I mean your girlfriend is sitting in jail right now, crying her eyes out, scared, alone and has no one to call to save her since you're here with me...for thirty-six hours if I wanted you."

"Thirty-six hours?" Fox frowned. "Man, where my lawyer?"

"Yea. Without charges, I can question you for up to thirty-six hours."

"You have no charges. What are you questioning me about?"

"Well, for one, where are the drugs you were supposed to deliver to Rev today? We didn't find them in your car."

"What drugs?" Fox replied.

"You know what drugs."

"I don't know what you're talking about," Fox played dumb.

"Perhaps they were the drugs we found in your girlfriend's trunk. In a black bag." Detective Johnson raised an eyebrow at Fox.

Fox froze as he was reminded that he did have drugs in Jasmine's car. "I still don't know what you're talking about."

"Cut the shit." The detective stood up quickly, angered. "Jasmine isn't exactly the type of girl to sell or transport drugs. You, on the other hand, we know you do. These were your drugs. If you don't make claim to them being yours, then she

144

will be sent to prison for a very long time. It wasn't a small amount of drugs in her car."

"Yo', you making all these claims and accusations and I don't know anything about this shit. I don't sell or transport shit. Y'all probably put that in her car!" Fox argued.

"You can claim YOUR drugs or watch her rot in jail. Choice is yours," Detective Johnson said, grabbed his folder and left the room.

Fox sucked his teeth and banged his hands down on the desk in frustration. He was between a rock and a hard place and he knew it. The moment the detective left the room, Fox knew it was only a matter of time before he returned with the same ultimatum. He had to make a decision.

What seemed like an eternity passed before the detective arrived back in the room. He strolled in with such arrogance that it made Fox sick. He sucked his teeth and rolled his eyes as he watched him come in and take a seat directly across from him again. He wasn't going to let the detective intimidate him. He sat and stared at him and gritted his teeth together. Fox wasn't going out like a bitch.

"So what is it going to be?" Detective Johnson said with a smirk.

"I don't know what you're talking about," Fox replied with the same cocky smirk.

"Are those your drugs we found in Jasmine's car?" Johnson clarified his question.

"No, I do not own any drugs," Fox said with a straight face.

"Ok. I gave you the choice to help her." Johnson shook his head, stood up and left the room.

On the other side of the station, the officers moved Jasmine into a room similar to where Fox was. She sat, shaking her leg nervously as she waited for the officers to return. She had no idea what was going on because this was all new to her. Naïve and clueless, she waited patiently, hoping they would just let her go.

This time, a detective arrived in the room and took a seat across from her. Her eyes red and wet from crying, he looked into them and felt disappointed. He knew the drugs belonged to Fox, but without any evidence of it, he had to book her for what was in her car. He wasn't surprised that Fox was cold hearted enough to let her go down for his stuff. He wasn't surprised at all.

"Listen, we have to charge you with possession with the intent to distribute," Detective Johnson told her.

"It's not mine! I don't sell drugs!" She sobbed even more.

"It was in your car, so the law says it belongs to you. Unless there is someone else who wants to claim them and so far, we have no one doing so."

"Can I talk to my boyfriend?" She wiped her nose and said in between cries.

"You had your phone calls. Is there anyone else you can call? Your boyfriend is actually in police custody."

"Is he here? Can I talk to him?" she begged.

"Normally, that's not allowed. I know this isn't something you're normally involved in, Jasmine. I do want to help you out," Detective Johnson tried to comfort her.

"Please, let me talk to him," Jasmine pleaded.

"Ok. I will bring him in here, and you will have just a few minutes to chat but after that, I'm going to have to formally charge you and place you into booking."

"Ok, thank you," Jasmine said with her head down. Even with a small victory of speaking to Fox, Jasmine's spirit was still defeated.

Fox arrived in the room and froze as soon as he saw Jasmine. He shut the door behind him and rushed to hug her. She cried in his arms as she tried to tell him what happened with the people trying to kidnap her first.

"Yo', shhh, don't say any more; I know they listening to us. Don't even talk about that." He lifted her face and kissed it.

"Baby, what am I going to do? That book bag in my trunk. They are saying it is mine and I'm getting charged with it unless someone claims it," Jasmine explained.

"What book bag?" Fox took a step back.

"The one I picked up for you," Jasmine said and stared at Fox.

"I don't know what you are talking about. I never asked you to pick up anything."

"Fox. It is not mine." Jasmine got annoyed.

"It ain't mine either. I don't know what you're even talking about," Fox played dumb.

"What? Fox, are you serious right now?" she screamed at Fox after realizing what was going on.

"Baby, calm down. I don't know anything about that," Fox said. "I will bail you out and get you a lawyer."

"You're lying, Fox! You're going to let me take this charge?" Jasmine began screaming. "You're going to deny it?" She ran towards him, swinging at him. He shielded his face from her blows, but caught a couple on the chin. The detective

147

ran in and pulled Jasmine off of him as he stepped back into the corner, further away from Fox so she couldn't hit him anymore.

"I can't believe you, Fox," she screamed as the detective dragged her out the room. He was disappointed that even in Jasmine's face, Fox still denied his involvement. Cold world, he thought to himself.

Back in the neighborhood, Jess was getting dressed and ready to head out to pick up the money where Jasmine said it was. She grabbed her keys and headed out to the school. In a short twenty minutes, she was inside and at the locker, using all her strength to cut the lock off. It took her another ten minutes to cut it, but she turned into Superwoman to get it off. The thought of how much money was in the locker motivated her to cut it. When she opened the locker and pulled out the four bags sitting inside, she could hardly contain her excitement.

She unzipped each one and stared at the green cash that was bundled inside of each bag. She dug into one of the bags to get an idea of how much was in each bag. Her mind couldn't even estimate how much it was. The bags were deep, but the cash ranged from singles, fives, tens, twenties and hundreds, making it hard for her to guess. After a few minutes of digging through the bag, she assumed it had to be something close to fifty thousand in each bag. She zipped it up quickly and lifted it onto her shoulder; it was heavier than she thought. It would take two trips. She dragged all four bags close to her exit point and got two out at a time and loaded them into her trunk. When she finally got all four bags into her car, she started her engine and drove off. She saw that she had three missed calls from the police station; she assumed it was Jasmine calling back. Just as she sat her phone down, it rang again with the same number.

"Hello?" Jess answered.

"Jess, it's Jasmine. Did you get the money? They're about to set my bail," Jasmine blurted into the phone.

"Girl, I went to where you said and there was no money in there. The lock was still there, but nothing was inside of the locker," Jess lied.

"Are you sure you went to the right locker?" Jasmine panicked.

"Yes, I triple checked."

"I don't get it. Why did he tell me it was there?"

"Maybe he took it out. Maybe he didn't trust you," Jess implied.

"He ain't shit!" Jasmine snapped.

"I tried to tell you that," Jess said.

"Yea, you did. I don't know what to do," Jasmine complained.

"Just let me know what you need me to do to help," Jess fake offered her concern.

"They just let Fox leave and I'm stuck here. I can't believe this! I need you to try to get me a lawyer."

"Do you have the money for one? How are you going to pay? You might need a public defender," Jess explained.

"I can't believe this," Jasmine cried as an officer rushed her off of the phone call.

Jess sped home and called her cell phone service provider. After being on hold for five minutes, she got someone on the line and requested to change her phone number. In a matter of minutes, she had a new number and was pulling up to her house. With the speed of light, she began packing all her belongings up in bags. She loaded all her stuff into her car and headed to her landlord's office. She paid to cancel her lease

149

and said her goodbyes to him. She warned him she left some furniture in the house and that he could sell it. He wasn't too happy about it, so she gave him some money for the removal and cleaning up of the place. She hopped back in her car and stopped at the gas station to fill up; she had a long drive ahead of her.

"Can you fill it up regular?" Jess asked the attendant.

"Sure," he answered and opened up her tank. His eyes wandered to her back seat full of luggage, clothes and shoes all stuffed in her car. "Moving?" he asked.

"Yup. Moving to Atlanta. Sometimes you just need a fresh start," Jess replied.

She smiled and drove off after paying for the gas. She turned the radio on and got onto the highway. She rolled the window down and let the air slap her in the face as she drove to wherever would be her new beginning in Atlanta. She didn't even think twice about robbing Fox or leaving Jasmine in jail. She knew she would find out where the money was at one way or another. Cold blooded with no fucks given, she sang along to the songs on the radio, as she drove towards her new home.

CPSIA information can be obtained
at www.ICGtesting.com
Printed in the USA
LVOW11s2227270217
525565LV00001B/134/P

9 781541 207448